Rolondo had seated himself again at the end of the examining table and was studying a scuff mark on one white shoe.

"Say," Rolondo said. "What happened to Mae West? I seen her leave here dead about a week ago. I was in here with one of my ladies, but you didn't see me. You was busy with Mae West."

"Mae West?"

"That ain't her real name, I know," Rolondo continued, "but that's what she went by. Kinky lady. You had the whole crowd in here with you, zapping her with wires, shooting her up. I never seen so many needles, even on the street."

St. Clair stopped and concentrated on what Rolondo was saying. "Are you talking about a white woman? Short black hair? Red wig?"

"That's her."

EMERGENCY MURDER

Janet McGiffin

FAWCETT GOLD MEDAL • NEW YORK

A Fawcett Gold Medal Book
Published by Ballantine Books
Copyright © 1992 by Janet Farber

All rights reserved under International and Pan-American Copyright Conventions. Published in the United States by Ballantine Books, a division of Random House, Inc., New York, and simultaneously in Canada by Random House of Canada Limited, Toronto.

Library of Congress Catalog Card Number: 91-75837

ISBN 0-449-14764-9

Manufactured in the United States of America

First Edition: February 1992

CHAPTER

1

IT WAS CLOSE to midnight on the Sunday after the Fourth, and St. Agnes Hospital emergency room was finally quiet. Dr. Maxene St. Clair sat sprawled in the ripped red plastic lounge chair in the supply room, taking a much needed break. Blood was smeared over the front of her white jacket. The left pocket had ripped when a wino with DTs had grabbed for it on his free-fall to the floor. A Betadine spill down the front of her summer cotton dress had left a terminal Rorschach stain.

A steady influx of knife wounds (kitchen knives as well as switchblades), inflamed appendices, high fevers of unknown origin, and drug-induced comas had kept Dr. St. Clair on her feet for most of her nine-hour shift. The sick and wounded from Milwaukee's steaming inner city, and from the less steaming but equally hot outer neighborhoods, had passed under her hands and were recuperating either up on the air-conditioned wards of St. Agnes' or back in some stifling flat.

The ER was empty except for Shirley Fitzgerald, RN, and a young nurse's aide who had been pulled off the wards to help clean up the debris. Stained paper covers lay crumpled under exam tables where they had been shoved with hurried hands as each new wave of wounded or sick was brought in and stretched out. Waste cans overflowed with used suture sets and blood-soaked gauze bandages. Articles of clothing lay forgotten on the floor and chairs, abandoned by bewildered or unconscious victims.

Shirley was yanking the antiseptic white-canvas curtains

away from around the gray exam tables where they had shrouded the sick and wounded since 3:00 that afternoon. Rushed doctors and nurses had pushed at the curtains, pulled at them, but never had time to fold them back against the walls and clean up the mounting debris.

Until now. The chains that connected the canvas to the metal grooves on the white ceiling zinged as Shirley whacked the curtains against the tile walls. Muscles bulged in Shirley's heavy black arms, and she panted heavily through her mouth, muttering dark epithets at the canvas.

The young nurse's aide flinched at each crack of canvas and moved her arms a trifle faster, pulling the rumpled and torn paper covers off the exam tables. She stuffed them all into the plastic garbage sacks, then began dumping in the contents of the waste cans, averting her face at an occasional malodorous bundle.

Joella, the Puerto Rican receptionist, rolled her dark and heavily made-up eyes at the crack, crack of canvas, but she didn't move any faster. She was stacking the shift's charts into two piles, one stack with admitting or discharge summaries for Dr. St. Clair to sign, and another stack that the doctor had somehow managed to sign during the hectic nine hours of the Sunday evening shift.

Dr. St. Clair was doing nothing. She sat, head back, eyes closed, in the red lounge chair. Her shoulders ached, her eyes burned, and her feet were puffed up like marshmallows. Midnight, end of shift, was fifteen minutes away. Should she down a cup of coffee to help her drive the twenty minutes to her flat on the east side? Or would the coffee just keep her awake when she got there?

Of course, she thought in a free-floating way, I can always crack open a Miller when I get home—beer counteracts caffeine every time. She was drifting off to sleep when someone picked up her limp right hand and placed a Styrofoam cup in it. She opened an eye. Coffee. "Thanks, Shirley."

"You never should have left that nice research job at the

university," Shirley said. "You gonna wear out before you even been here a year."

Shirley pulled a metal chair into the supply room doorway so she could watch the outer emergency room for any new patients. The chair creaked under her bulk. Her support hose cut valleys into the rolls of flesh below her knees.

"Maybe thirty-eight is just too old to be an ER doc," St. Clair said, closing her eyes again. "Sister Rosalie says the ER doctors don't work hard enough, that the patients come in bunches, then there's none for a while. She's talking about putting me on call for the wards, too."

"Sister Rosalie wants the bishop to think she knows how to run a hospital. She's full of the stuff that runs downhill. Ignore her."

"Ignoring Sister Rosalie is like ignoring Rolondo when he's brought in one of his ladies to be sewed up."

"You're too nice to that pimp."

"He pays his hookers' bills in cash. That's better than Medicare."

"He should keep them girls from getting banged up. That's what pimps are for." Shirley kicked off her shoes and hiked up her stockings. Then she groaned. "Hell. Speaking of hookers, here comes another one. When will they learn not to pick up men that beat on them?"

Maxene St. Clair leaned forward in her chair and peered around the corner of the door, past the nurse's station and the admitting desk where Joella was still stacking charts. The electric doors slid open with a menacing hiss. A taxi driver in a sweat-soaked T-shirt was standing in the doorway, his greasy cap pushed to the back of his head. Draped over his tattooed arm like a rag doll hung a white woman. Her black leather miniskirt was stretched tight across her hips, and her sleeveless pink sweater hugged the rest of her body, making it obvious she wore nothing underneath.

The taxi driver shifted her to the other arm. As he did, the woman's blazing red wig fell off, showing spiky black hair matted with sweat. The wig lay on the floor like a puddle of blood. The woman lifted her head. Her eyes, rimmed with tear-smeared mascara, roamed the antiseptic whiteness.

"Maxene," she moaned. "Where's Maxene?"

St. Clair jumped to her feet, coffee splashing to the floor. "That's no hooker!" she cried. "That's Nanette Myer— Hank Myer's wife!" She ran to catch the woman as the taxi driver let her slither to the floor.

"Hank Myer, the surgeon?" Shirley panted, right behind her. "You sure? She doesn't smell like a doctor's wife." Shirley caught the woman under the knees, and together they lifted her limp body onto an exam table. The smell of perfumed sweat rose in waves.

Dr. St. Clair was having trouble believing it herself. She stared down at the gasping figure on the exam table. Hank Myer was a hard-driving, fast-talking surgeon who had his finger in every piece of medical politics in Milwaukee. He had a big private practice, was on the staff of five hospitals, and sat on the Board of Regents at the Medical College of Wisconsin. He lived in a white brick mansion on North Lake Drive—light-years from the St. Agnes inner-city ER. What was his wife doing here?

"Can't breathe," Nanette whispered. She shook like a beaten dog.

"Sit her up," Dr. St. Clair ordered, taking an elbow. The tanned arm was slippery with sweat.

Shirley pulled her upright. They balanced her at the end of the exam table, her marionette-thin legs dangling disjointedly over the end.

Maxene felt herself becoming unprofessionally alarmed. She couldn't see the problem. Nanette had no bruises or blood. She wasn't holding herself in pain. Maybe she was just badly frightened. But what was she doing in those clothes? "When did this all start, Nanette?" she demanded.

"A few minutes ago. A taxi stopped for me, thank God."

"Ever had anything like this before?"

"No. Help me! I can't breathe. I feel sick. Everything's blurry." She gulped air like it was water.

"Are you taking any medications?"

"In my purse." She groped toward the black leather satchel that Joella had taken from the taxi driver. The bag fell to the floor. A rolled-up paisley caftan spilled out.

Shirley pushed it aside and dug through the purse, laying pill bottles out on the exam table. "Valium, five milligrams; Elavil, fifteen milligrams; tetracycline, a hundred and fifty milligrams; vitamin B complex. Do all doctor's wives take this much medicine?"

St. Clair had been taking Nanette's blood pressure, letting Nanette lean all her weight against her. Nanette's head drooped on her shoulder. St. Clair shook the limp arm. "Where have you been tonight? What did you eat?"

Nanette clutched suddenly at Maxene's hand and gulped air. "I thought it was an antibiotic," she whimpered. "That's what the other pills were, I'm sure."

"What other pills? These?"

Nanette didn't answer. Her head hung forward. Maxene and Shirley stretched the woman out on her back. Maxene pulled out her stethoscope. Nanette's heart sounded fine, just a slight normal systolic murmur. Her lungs were clear. Her stomach was soft with no sign of infection. She could move her neck, arms, and legs equally well, but they seemed weak.

Nanette started gasping. "I can't see!" she shrieked, her voice shaking in panic. "It's all dark!"

Maxene pulled up an eyelid. The pupils were equal in size, but they were not holding straight. Her lids and her face muscles drooped, as did the corners of her mouth. She gagged weakly when St. Clair looked down her throat with the tongue blade.

St. Clair tapped on the tendon on the side of Nanette's hand with her percussion hammer. "Reflexes are depressed," she murmured, frowning. She was pulling off one of Nanette's scuffed four-inch spike heels to run her finger up the sole of her foot to test for the Babinski reflex when Nanette stopped breathing and went limp.

"Doctor! No pulse in her neck!" Shirley snapped.

"Call Code Red!" Dr. St. Clair shouted to Joella. Maxene felt for the sternum with her left hand, then smashed her fist down on it, hoping to depolarize the heart and start it beating again.

Shirley had started mouth-to-mouth resuscitation. Joella was calling Code Red over the paging system. In a minute, a running crowd of white-jacketed specialists would hurtle through the swinging doors from the hospital, pushing a cart loaded with instruments representing every medical advancement of the century.

Nanette Myer would stop being a person and would become a system of symptoms, each treated separately until either the symptoms persisted into death, or the entire system returned to life. Then the system of symptoms would stop being a naked object lying on the table with needles and tubes sticking from all sides and become again Nanette Myer, who could say why and how she got into this condition.

Feet pounded in the hall. The doors crashed open and hospital personnel hurtled a cart into the ER, up next to the exam table where Nanette was lying. They began pulling instruments and tubes off the cart. Dr. St. Clair stood back to direct the operations.

A nurse slid a respirator mask over Nanette's face and started squeezing a black rubber bag attached to the mask, rhythmically pushing air into Nanette's mouth and nose, thirteen breaths per minute. An intern scrambled onto the table. He knelt by the body, leaning on the chest with his hands placed one over the other. He started leaning all his weight on and off, on and off, seventy-two compressions on the heart per minute.

Another nurse was cutting the thin pink pullover up the front with a pair of bent, blunt-tipped surgical scissors. She tucked the scissors into her pocket and peeled off the pink sweater from under the intern's hands. Then she began taping electrical patches onto the chest between the intern's fingers. The patches were connected to wires attached to the EKG monitor on the cart.

Shirley was starting an IV, pushing a needle into the already collapsing vein on the inside of Nanette's elbow. She hooked the needle to a tube leading to a plastic bag of fluid hanging from a standard. She adjusted the drip of fluid from the bag by closing a valve on the tube. Then she picked up the clipboard to write down every symptom, every medication, every medical action.

"Pupils still mid-position and normal," St. Clair said to Shirley, who made a note. She relaxed slightly and looked up at the heart monitor screen. Not normal. The heart had started beating by itself, but out of control. "Ventricular fib," she said. "Defibrillator. Four hundred watt seconds."

Dr. St. Clair moved to stand close to the chest and held out her hands for the instruments. The nurse spread clear jelly onto electrical paddles, then smacked the handles into Maxene's palms. The intern climbed off the table. Maxene placed one paddle over the upper right chest, the other over the left lower.

"Everybody stand clear." She checked her own body to make sure she was not touching anything metal, then pressed the button in the handle of the right paddle.

There was a popping noise and a charred smell. The body jerked convulsively.

"Still V-fib," Dr. St. Clair said, eyes on the monitor. "Recharge." No heartbeat at all. "Asystole," she said. "Back to cardiac massage."

It seemed like hours were passing, yet it all had taken place in about thirty seconds.

"Intracardiac Adrenalin."

A nurse thrust the syringe with Adrenalin into Dr. St. Clair's hand instantly, as if she had been waiting for the order. Dr. St. Clair counted down four ribs, then plunged the five-inch needle in at an angle toward the heart. Bright red blood squirted back up into the syringe.

"She's getting air from somewhere," the intern muttered.

Maxene pushed down the plunger. Ten cc's of Adrenalin swirling with the blood slid into the heart.

"Still no pulse in her neck," a nurse said. "Pupils beginning to dilate." The intern climbed back on the table and began pushing, resting, pushing, resting, on the chest, compressing the heart.

"Intubate," Dr. St. Clair ordered. It seemed as if someone other than she was making the decisions. Progression from one stage of therapy to the next was automatic.

"Stop CPR. Assess rhythm."

A nurse's voice called out, "Still asystole." She slid the respirator mask off the face and tilted back the head. Dr. St. Clair slid the laryngoscope easily down the throat. She stopped pushing when she got a good view of the vocal cords. Then she slid the endotracheal tube along the same route, but farther down the trachea into the lungs. She used a syringe loaded with air to blow up a cuff in the throat to prevent the endotracheal tube from coming out. The nurse attached the ambu bag directly to the endotracheal tube and started pumping air directly into the lungs.

"Air going into the lungs," the intern said, his stethoscope on the chest. He climbed back on the table and started leaning on the chest wall again.

Dr. St. Clair looked at her watch. A little over one minute had passed since she had injected Adrenalin into the heart. CPR had stopped only for ten seconds while the endotracheal tube was inserted.

"Still no independent heartbeat," the nurse said.

"Let's try another ampule of Adrenalin," said Dr. St. Clair.

Again the needle into the heart. Still no independent heartbeat.

"Transthoracic pacemaker." During her years in training, she had seen this pacemaker work only once, but it was worth a last-ditch effort, especially with such a young woman. While the nurse was preparing the syringe, Dr. St. Clair pulled up a half-closed eyelid. Dread crept into her heart. The pupils were getting larger. Why? Nanette was getting enough air. She was getting enough fluids. Her heart was being compressed, and blood was getting to her brain. Why was the brain going dead?

The RN handed her the large trochar—a sheath of metal like an enormous needle with a solid metal needle inside that would be inserted into the heart. The trochar and needle would go in together, then the needle would be withdrawn and the fragile pacemaker wires threaded into place.

The trochar slid in easily, followed by the needle and pacemaker wires. Dr. St. Clair withdrew the inside needle, attached a syringe to the trochar, and drew out blood enough for later tests, if needed. She handed the syringe filled with bright red blood to the nurse.

"Send this to the lab for electrolytes, pH, and glucose."

Pacemaker wires in place, the intern taped them to the chest wall, then hooked the other ends of the wires to the pacemaker monitor that would send an electrical impulse to the heart at prescribed intervals, keeping the heart beating artificially. She set the threshold at one mili-amp of electricity and set the rate at eighty beats per minute. She flipped on the monitor switch.

Electrical activity. "Paced beat of eighty beats per minute," Dr. St. Clair said. "Still no neck pulse. Start external heart massage again."

The intern climbed onto the table and placed the heels of his hands over the sternum. Lean, rest, lean, rest.

Fifteen minutes had passed. "Off pacemaker," Dr. St. Clair ordered. "Inject twenty-five grams of glucose into the IV line and inject calcium gluconate into the heart wall."

The nurse slid the needle into the IV and pushed the plunger.

Dr. St. Clair was about to do the same into the heart wall when she saw that Reginald Giardelli, a cardiologist, had arrived and was reading the progress notes over Shirley's shoulder. Maxene stepped back from the body and quickly filled him in.

Giardelli nodded, no comment. From him, a real pat on the back. He reached for the syringe and took charge, his prerogative as specialist. He injected the calcium gluconate into the heart wall. All eyes to the monitor. No change. The intern climbed wearily back onto the table.

Five minutes passed, while everyone watched the intern, visibly tired, compressing the heart wall. Giardelli held up a hand like a traffic cop. He ordered CPR stopped. Again, everyone looked at the monitor. No pulse. Only pacemaker activity on the monitor.

Maxene placed her hand over the half-closed eyes and drew back the eyelids. She closed them again. The pupils were dilated. Brain damage.

Giardelli grunted under his breath. He moved to the foot of the table and pulled a spiked heel off the dirty bare foot. He ran a finger up the sole of the foot. The toes spread apart, positive sign of permanent brain damage.

Shirley tightened her lips.

Giardelli fiddled with the pacemaker, getting no independent activity from the heart. It refused to beat.

"Call the code," he said, and shook his head. He dropped the syringe onto the tray and turned away. The intern climbed off the table, straightened his rumpled jacket and pants, and hurried to catch up with the cardiologist.

The nurse who had been squeezing the black bellows dropped her arm to her side and let it dangle for a few seconds. Then she shook it and began peeling the bag off the tube. She tossed the black bag onto the crash cart. Then she pulled back on the plunger of the syringe that had pumped air into the cuff that held the endotracheal tube in place inside the throat, and slowly pulled the tube out of the useless lung. She dropped it into a plastic trash bag that Shirley was holding. Then she disconnected the IV tube, pulled the needle out of the bruised and limp arm, and dropped that into the same bag.

The second nurse picked up a clipboard and began making check marks on a list of all the supplies that had been used—needles, plastic tubing, IV bag, even the four plastic patches that held the EKG wire in place on the now quiet chest. She went methodically down the list, pointing silently at items lying on the exam table, on the body, on the crash cart. The other nurse tossed them into the plastic bag.

Finally the list was complete. The nurse unclipped it from the clipboard and handed it to Shirley, who attached that list to the ER chart. It would be included in the final bill sent to the insurance company.

The two nurses nodded to Shirley, then began wheeling the crash cart toward the double doors into the hospital. As they reached the doors, they began to chat.

Shirley finished writing, noted time of death, and signed the page. She pulled a blue cotton sheet from the supply shelf under the table and unfolded it over the body. Legs covered, body covered, face covered.

"Call an orderly," she said to Joella. "Body to the morgue."

Dr. St. Clair just stood and watched.

CHAPTER

2

WHAT WAS RINGING? Code Red? Burglar alarm? The luminous green of the digital clock leered at St. Clair through a murky haze. The numbers blurred, cleared, 3:16 A.M.

"Yes? Hello?" Maxene mumbled.

"Hank Myer here. I'm in Chicago." His voice, harsh but with an underlying quaver, cleared her misted brain. Maxene sat up, posture further draining away sleep. She had tried to locate Hank until 1:30. All she could learn by phoning his answering service and the other doctors in his clinic was that he was in Chicago at a conference. No one knew which conference or what hotel. Finally, she got the home phone number of his office nurse. By then, St. Clair was hoarse with fatigue. Her tongue had felt numb.

"Nanette Myer came into St. Agnes ER tonight and died suddenly," was all she had been able to manage. Brevity hadn't mattered; the nurse took over with brisk efficiency.

"I'll call Dr. Myer. He'll call you back."

Driving home at 2:00 A.M. she kept reviewing the details of the death. Fast pulse, high blood pressure, but neither would cause heart attack. How could a thirty-five-year-old woman with no history of heart problems suddenly drop dead of heart failure? St. Clair kept worrying she had missed something during the exam, overlooked a symptom. Worry gnawed at her. She had been mentally going over the symptoms when her head hit the pillow and she fell asleep. Falling asleep in a minute was a skill she had developed during internship. Waking up quickly was another.

She switched on the oriental lamp by the bed. Its soft light blotted out the eerie green of the clock.

"Hank. I'm so glad you called me. Did your nurse tell you about your wife?"

"Yes, but I don't understand. What happened?" Professional, cold. Yet the force of him transmitted over the line. He seemed to be standing by her bed, not a hundred miles away.

"She came in at eleven-thirty with symptoms of respiratory distress, fatigue, nausea, neurological deficits. During the exam, she arrested. Reg Giardelli was in house, and we did everything we could, but her heart just stopped."

"What do you mean, her heart? There was nothing wrong with her heart, aside from a slight congenital murmur." His voice shook.

Maxene waited to let him get himself under control. "I don't understand it either. What about autopsy?"

The seconds ticked by. Autopsy was required for undefined death, and he knew it.

"Who will do it?" he asked, finally.

"I can ask Simonson."

She waited out another silence.

"What was Nanette doing at St. Agnes ER?" he said. "That's in the inner city."

"She called out my name as soon as she got inside. Maybe she came because I was there. We could ask the taxi driver."

"Taxi? What happened to her car? Why was she in a taxi?"

"She was too sick for me to ask. But Hank."

"What?"

St. Clair hesitated, uncertain whether to tell him that his wife had come in wearing the red wig and tight clothes of a hooker. He would find out if he looked into the sack with her personal effects. But what if he didn't look? Telling patients and family the bald truth was always the best policy, St. Clair had found during her years of medical training. The truth came out eventually; better sooner than later. "Hank, when Nanette came in, she was wearing a leather miniskirt."

"So?"

"And a red wig."

"What are you talking about?" His voice sounded worn, defeated.

"Nothing. It's not important. We can talk about it later."

Maxene hung up slowly and switched off the light. She could still hear Myer's voice in her ears, feel his presence. The man had a physical effect on her—and on everyone else, it seemed. Whenever she was with him, whether it was at a university function or just in St. Agnes cafeteria during lunch, Hank filled the space around him more fully than other people. He exuded power, which either attracted people or frightened them away. To Maxene's own embarrassment, she was one of the group who was attracted. She wasn't sure, however, whether it was the power or the flattering attention he paid to her. He had listened sympathetically to her during the long foolish months of her divorce. It had seemed natural to turn to him for help. In the end, he had given her more than help. He had given her his affection and returned to her the self-respect ground under by the divorce struggle.

In the dark, she could hear Ruby crunching her cat chow in the kitchen. The noise was sinister. As she drifted back to sleep, images of the last time she had seen Nanette Myer spun through her brain. It had been at a pool party at the Myer's massive brick colonial that sat on a bluff overlooking Lake Michigan. The long, curved driveway was lined with Porsches, Mercedeses, Corvettes. It was the usual doctor crowd—half of them academics from the Medical College of Wisconsin, and half physicians in private practice. Maxene had a foot in both camps. She had spent six years teaching and doing research at the Medical College, and now she was an ER doctor.

She parked her yellow Nissan outside the gates and followed a herringbone brick path across the sculptured lawn and around the corner of the house.

The pool was on the south side, sheltered between the library wing and the main house. Clipped fir hedges cut the cool evening breeze off the lake. It was a languid Midwest evening, iced gin and tonics sliding down one after the other, soft music from the house, a few people dancing in the shadows. Maxene snapped some photos while it was still light. Photography was her only hobby, and she took occasional classes at the vocational school to make sure she didn't lose touch with life outside medicine. Her photos weren't bad, usually. She put them in with Christmas cards she sent to the friends who appeared in the photos—a personal touch people seemed to like.

Nanette was lounging on the other side of the pool, her high-pitched laughter shrill. Her black hair matched her silk jumpsuit, the scarlet sash gleaming in the torchlight. The luminescent blue of the pool grew stronger as the day faded. The pool lit everyone's faces from below. Evening moved into night as smoothly as the gin slid down her throat.

Maxene hadn't realized how much she had drunk until she tried to stand. The torchlights blurred, the chair seemed to tilt, and she dropped back onto the cushions, giving it up as a bad idea. Hank had appeared from the darkness behind her like a satyr. He slipped a fresh drink into her hand, letting his fingers linger over hers. Then he pulled a chair close and squeezed her arm.

"You enjoying your divorce?" he murmured.

"Did I ever thank you for all your moral support?"

"What are friends for?" He took her hand and held it tightly.

Maxene glanced at Nanette across the blue pool. She eased her hand away. "Your wife gives good parties. She says you arrived with the guests."

"My secretary arranged this party, not Nanette. The service is part of Nanette's pot of gold at the end of the rainbow, when I finished surgical training and she had all the money she could ever want." He tossed off his drink.

"Some doctors' wives say all they want is a husband at home instead of one who loiters around hospitals."

"And others settle for this." He waved an arm.

His words hung in St. Clair's ears as she dropped back to sleep. Ruby let her sleep until noon. She got her own breakfast by ripping open a chicken breast thawing in the sink.

"You cats are like humans," Maxene chided her as she gathered up the half-chewed bones. "Never civilized—just pretend to be."

By the time she got to the ER at 3:00, the sterile hospital whiteness was already filled with groaning or bleeding people and an orderly was wheeling in another gurney to hold the overflow. Summer in the city meant people trying to destroy themselves with cars, knives, firecrackers. About 9:00 P.M. a phone call interrupted Maxene bandaging a small boy's knee. She turned the job over to Shirley. Aaron Simonson was calling from Pathology.

"Nanette Myer's autopsy was negative," he said. He took a bite of something crunchy.

"That's all? I was hoping for something more definite."

"Heart failure."

"And the pills? The tetracycline?"

"Just what the labels said. I had every one analyzed. All standard prescriptions. She didn't even show signs of allergic reaction."

Shirley was waving a chart at her. Two gurneys that had been empty when Maxene had picked up the phone were now occupied by what looked like car accident victims.

"I'm filling up here, Aaron. Thanks for telling me."

He didn't hang up. "Did you know Nanette well?" he asked.

"I knew Hank better, from when I was at the university. But I went to a couple of parties at their house. There was one last weekend. You were there, too, remember?"

"Was I? All I remember is waking up Sunday with a blinding headache."

An hour later, the ER was empty again, accident victims rolled off to surgery. St. Clair finished charting, cleaned blood off her skirt with fingernail polish remover, and sat down in the ripped lounge chair to sip acrid coffee. Shirley dragged her chair into the doorway vantage point.

"The Myer autopsy said heart failure, I heard," Shirley said. "You really think a young woman like that can up and die of heart failure?"

"She came in with those symptoms, I did what I could, and she died anyway." Tension and fatigue were taking their toll on her patience. She stopped, embarrassed. Losing her temper was something she had vowed never to do. She'd seen enough raging surgeons throwing instruments—Hank Myer included.

"Dr. Myer is a handsome dude," Shirley said, reading her mind. "Powerful sense of himself as man in charge. He throws ripples in the nursing staff every time he walks through the wards." She picked up the ringing phone and handed it over. It was Hank Myer's nurse.

"The funeral for Mrs. Myer will be at Brentwood Cemetery tomorrow morning at eleven," said the cool, impersonal voice. "Dr. Myer asked me to call you personally."

Maxene hung up with a feeling of resignation. She dreaded funerals, especially those of her own patients. "The funeral is tomorrow," she sighed. "Dr. Myer wanted me to know."

Shirley raised an eyebrow.

CHAPTER

3

NANETTE MYER WAS buried in a grassy cemetery so shaded by elms and maples that dew still clung to the grass by the open grave. Sparrows rustled the foliage and a meadowlark warbled from a hedge, drowning the faint wail of a faraway siren. A breeze off Lake Michigan half a mile east relieved the sultry press of July heat. The mourners were doctors and wives, dressed in raw silk suits of subdued gray or beige. A tearless crowd, more curious than sad, performing their professional duty.

I hate funerals, Maxene thought, wishing she had worn something other than her usual cotton print dress. She stretched her shoulders discreetly, to ease the feeling she was carrying a forty-pound pack. Heat normally didn't affect her, so the backache must come from the knowledge that she had presided over the death of the person now being buried.

Hank Myer stood in front, separated from her by an irregular line of people. His suntanned neck and carefully trimmed hair made her feel inexplicably sad, for herself as much as for him. Funerals were lonely, made even lonelier by memories of other cemeteries, other funerals. She remembered again the small funeral of her aunt, a doctor who had spent her medical life in small village hospitals in India. Her aunt had outlived all her friends, and Maxene had been her only link to the profession to which she had given her heart. Her passion for healing had been Maxene's reason for becoming a doctor—at least at the beginning. By the time Maxene had graduated, the passion was dampened by the medical training process and replaced by scientific curiosity—the reason she ended up in research. Maxene missed her aunt very much, especially at funerals.

The catered reception after the funeral was at the Myer house. It was another crowd scene, loud this time, inside air-conditioned, designer-decorated rooms. Maxene pushed past the noisy group at the buffet table and wandered into the library. Mahogany bookshelves stood against walls dressed in the same delicate Chinese fabric as the drapes and deep-cushioned armchairs. Behind the black-lacquered piano, French doors led outside to a birdbath. The enormous pool glistened in the noon sun. St. Clair was absorbing the cool elegance when she felt a hand on her elbow and smelled a familiar perfume.

"Virginia!" she exclaimed. "I didn't see you at the funeral."

"You were too busy watching Hank Myer, dear. Try to be less obvious. People might think you had something going. Or should I say, still had something going?"

"I was simply paying attention to the service." Maxene tried not to sound horrified. Virginia Gaust had a frightening habit of noticing everything that went on around her and commenting on it without hesitation, as Maxene had learned when she shared a lab with Virginia at Marquette University. Like St. Clair, Dr. Gaust was on the faculty at the Medical College, and had her office and lab at the Marquette pharmacology building. Unlike St. Clair, however, Virginia was still there. How she had managed to rise to department head in academic medicine at age forty-five was a tribute to her brains, not her mouth. Dr. Gaust's research was brilliant and was funded by a big European drug firm, but her real passion was gossip. Maxene had tried to keep the sordid details of her divorce away from Virginia's prying ears, but Virginia learned everything anyway. Probably from Maxene's ex-husband. Whether Virginia knew about Hank's warm support during Maxene's divorce was more than Maxene wanted to think about.

Virginia plunked a plate of cucumber sandwiches onto the gleaming library table and waved Maxene to the opposite chair.

"Where have you been hiding since you left the Medical College?" she demanded, handing over a cucumber sandwich. "For six months I've been leaving messages all over St. Agnes. I thought maybe you died." She glanced furtively at the doorway and lowered her voice.

Maxene nibbled at the crunchy bittersweet sandwich. "By the time midnight rolls around, I'm in no condition to return anyone's calls."

"What do you do besides work? Surely divorce hasn't soured you on sex? You should never have married Alan, dear. I told you that at the time. You had all the men you could handle."

"I've been divorced less than a year, Virginia. Give me time. Besides, I'm busy learning to be an ER doctor. After six years in research, I'd forgotten the sound of a heartbeat."

"I still don't understand why you quit your very promising research because of a silly divorce. Alan isn't even at the Medical College anymore."

"I didn't quit, Virginia. I just took a year's leave. My research grant is still waiting. In six months I'll be back."

Virginia didn't take a breath before plunging into another touchy subject. "I heard you were the ER doctor when Nanette died. Tell me, was she really dressed like a hooker?"

Maxene looked around. Virginia's voice carried like a foghorn. "Where did you hear that?"

"Hospitals are no place for secrets, dear. You should know that after what happened with your husband. I never did figure out what he saw in that little chemistry student."

St. Clair ground her teeth.

Virginia chattered on. "I also heard Nanette died of heart failure. Unusual for such a young woman. Was that the real diagnosis?"

"Of course it was the real diagnosis. Sister Rosalie doesn't look kindly on ER doctors who misrepresent diagnoses on charts," Maxene said stiffly. "But I have to admit that I'm not one hundred percent sure I was right. Nanette walked in out of nowhere and arrested before I even finished taking the medical history. I've never seen anything like it."

"Sounds odd." Virginia nodded. "But heart failure can present itself in a lot of ways."

"Too odd," Maxene said. "Like I said, I'm less and less sure of the diagnosis."

"Why? Because of the way she was dressed? Or did Nanette tell you something before she died?"

St. Clair frowned, trying to remember. "She didn't say anything significant. She mumbled something about an antibiotic, but Aaron Simonson in Pathology had the tetracycline in her purse analyzed, and the pills were all standard prescription. She didn't say why she was taking them. I also wish I knew why she was wearing those bizarre clothes." St. Clair leaned forward and lowered her voice. "Have you heard any gossip about what Nanette was doing that night?"

"Not a word," Virginia said promptly. "But let me tell you one thing: if you keep eyeing Hank Myer like he was a male stripper, I'm bound to hear something about you."

A swarm of mourners moving toward the front door drowned St. Clair's protest. Doctors were hurrying back to clinics before their waiting rooms filled up with impatient patients. St. Clair shoved what remained of her cucumber sandwich into her mouth and joined the line of people extending their sympathy to Hank as they hurried out the door.

Hank Myer's face was pale and his eyes red. A tick jerked the skin over one cheek. He held Maxene's hands hard for a long moment. On sudden impulse, she kissed his cheek.

"I'll call you," she promised. She hurried out the door into the blazing sun.

Ahead of her, caning his way carefully down the herringbone brick walk through the rose beds, was a familiar figure from Marquette University, Stan Litwack, past chair of the department of pharmacology. He stopped to sniff a

Queen Elizabeth rose, his frail shoulders bent from decades of crouching over microscopes.

"Stanley," Maxene said, taking his arm. "I need to talk."

Despite his long tenure, Stan Litwack still spent more time in the classroom than any professor at Marquette. He was an easy man to talk to; he sat back relaxed in his creaking wooden chair, ignoring his ringing phone and paying flattering attention to whoever climbed over the piles of books and found an empty chair. During her years at Marquette, St. Clair had spent countless hours talking out her research. She had also talked out her life. Stanley's quiet interest reminded her of her aunt, whose death had left Maxene without a confidant or mentor. She found a partial substitute in Stanley.

"You're worried about Nanette Myer's death," Stanley hazarded, as he drove his ancient Mercedes the few blocks to Atwood Beach parking lot. They sat on a park bench on the bluff, looking down at the shining white sand far below. Bright-colored umbrellas mushroomed. Children ran through the knee-high waves, kicking water into glittering arcs. A cool breeze brought summer smells—hot dogs, mosquito repellent, freedom.

"There's something wrong, but I don't know what or even how to start looking," St. Clair began. "It's like trying to use a microscope that doesn't have a light. Nanette Myer's autopsy came back 'heart failure,' but I think she died of more than that. I just don't know what."

A flock of seagulls settled on the grass waiting for handouts. They had all left by the time St. Clair finished describing the symptoms, treatment, her failure. Stanley knocked the ashes of his pipe out onto the grass.

"I've been out of the world of diagnosis for a long time," he said, "but pharmacology being my specialty, I can make a couple of guesses. From the abrupt onset of symptoms and the sudden shutdown of all systems, starting with the neurological, it sounds to me like poison."

"Poison!" St. Clair lowered her voice, a big effort. "Not possible. Autopsy was negative."

Stanley had the half-humored look that he wore when graduate students omitted vital lab experiments. "Did the pathologist test for neurotoxins? There are plenty of obscure ones that won't show up unless you test for them specifically. You know one, yourself. What's that stuff you were messing around with for years?"

"Tetrodotoxin? What has that to do with Nanette Myer?"

"Haven't I heard you talking about its effect on heart muscle? And the effects on the neurosystem? Autopsy would be negative, of course. No one in this part of the country would think to test for it, since it's so rare."

"Absurd, Stanley. Tetrodotoxin is a research drug. How would Nanette get it?"

"All right then, curare. Or rattlesnake venom."

"How would Nanette Myer get into any of those? You don't find those drugs by accident, especially when you're in the middle of Milwaukee's inner city on a Sunday night."

"I can't speculate on how she ingested the drug, Maxene. It's moot anyway until you figure out which drug killed her."

"If it was a drug," she said stubbornly.

He shrugged. "Find out."

"How? She's buried. We were just at her funeral."

"Dig her up. Or find out if whoever did the autopsy saved blood or tissue. But first, Maxene," and Stanley shook a careful finger at her, "decide if this is the right research for you to be doing. How important is finding out how she died? The authorities are satisfied. Hank Myer seems satisfied. Maybe Nanette Myer should be left in peace."

St. Clair thought that over as she made the trek from shady cool suburb to boiling inner city and the refrigerated bowels of St. Agnes. How important was it to find how Nanette Myer died so suddenly and horribly? Who wanted her death cleared up?

Did Hank? Hank hadn't said anything more about finding cause of death, but they had only spoken of it once, on the phone.

Who else cared why Nanette Myer died? You do, said a voice inside her head. Nanette Myer came to the ER calling your name, asking for your help. And you failed her. Did you do all you could? What really killed her? Was it you?

And then, of course, she had to admit to the underlying curiosity about disease and illness that obsesses every doctor, especially a doctor who is also a Ph.D. involved in medical research. Nanette Myer's death was an unexplained medical event that might be answered by an intelligent person applying systematic and persistent research methods. An M.D., Ph.D. like Maxene St. Clair.

She hurried through the automatic doors of St. Agnes ER at 2:45, with just enough time to talk to Aaron Simonson in Pathology.

Aaron was keeping company with a partially disemboweled corpse. He looked up as Maxene pushed open the double swinging doors and waved a friendly scalpel. A green mask covered his fat cheeks, and layers of green surgical gowns shrouded his chubby body. St. Clair kept her distance. Who knew what disease had killed the person under his knife?

"I need a favor," she said. "Another look at Nanette Myer's autopsy."

"File's in the cabinet, top drawer." The words were muffled by the mask.

"Not the paperwork—the blood work. I think Nanette was poisoned by something you may not have tested for."

Aaron stopped slicing away a body organ and let his gloved hands rest inside the body cavity. "Poisoned!" he exclaimed. "What with?"

"A neurotoxin, like tetrodotoxin."

Aaron's eyebrows raised, and he chuckled. "Why not pit viper venom? Or curare. Curare is a whole lot more available to the average Midwestern poisoner than tetrowhatever. Just rob an undergraduate anatomy lab before the students use up their curare on helpless frogs."

"Okay, curare. Test for something that produces the same symptoms that Nanette Myer died with," St. Clair said stubbornly. "Tetrodotoxin poisoning fits those symptoms. I know because I did research with it when I was at Marquette. I'm not happy with heart failure as an autopsy finding, Aaron. I think we should keep looking."

Simonson slid a new blade into his scalpel. "Why, Max? Everyone else is happy with the finding. Even Hank."

"There's no logical reason why a thirty-five-year-old woman should die of heart failure."

"Worried you didn't handle it right? Be careful, Max. A second autopsy with positive findings could drag you into malpractice court. I don't think Hank would sue you—he's made his share of fatal errors, like all of us—but what about Nanette's family?"

"I don't remember any family at the funeral, and I still want you to go ahead with more lab tests."

Simonson began cutting away at the body on the table. "You know Hank pretty well," he commented.

Maxene gritted her teeth. Had Aaron seen her ogling Hank Myer at the funeral, as Virginia put it? "I know him very casually," she lied, sounding defensive even to herself. She changed the subject briskly. "What do we do now? Exhume the body for tissue samples?"

"No," said Simonson, "even if that were possible after an embalmer gets through with his work. As luck would have it, I saved blood and tissue samples from the Myer autopsy. They're in the freezer."

"You always keep blood samples from autopsies?"

"Just inconclusive autopsies. I wish I had a nickel for all the times the cops came in here two months after a death and said, 'Let's start over.' I used to tell them that results may be inaccurate because blood and tissue deteriorate over time, but I found it's easier to keep samples and do what they want."

"How long will it take to run the tests?"

"I have to send them to the Armed Forces Institute of Pathology, in Texas. I'll put a sample in the mail today."

"I owe you one, Aaron."

"You certainly do, sweetheart. And Maxene."

She stopped, hand on the swinging door.

"Please realize what this may get you into. If we find that Nanette Myer was poisoned by your research drug, you might find yourself answering some tricky questions about your lab techniques, as well as your emergency room diagnostic abilities. ER doctors lose their jobs by missing diagnoses as easily as professors lose theirs when their research chemicals cause fatalities. You could find yourself out of a job here, with no academic career to go back to."

The conversation occupied her mind through the nine-hour shift and during the warm drive across the Milwaukee River into the east side neighborhoods. She even forgot to feel guilty when she crossed into that cleaner, quieter, greener world beyond the inner city.

The flat she had rented after her divorce was on the upper floor of a typical two-story Milwaukee brown frame bungalow, set at the same prescribed distance from the street as all the other bungalows on the block. The small front porch had two identical glass paneled front doors and two identical mail slots. There the similarity ended.

Downstairs was starkly art nouveau, the personality of her antique-store neighbor who spent all his earnings on art. Upstairs, her apartment was furnished with the faded treasures brought back from India by her aunt. There was a well-worn but nice blue Sarouk on the floor, a blue-and-coral striped wingback and footstool, a sky blue couch flanked by small tables inlaid with semiprecious stones, and two tall Chinese lamps. St. Clair had moved the whole ensemble three times—once from her apartment before she was married, once briefly to Alan's place, and now here.

Maxene pulled up in front of her bungalow and turned off the motor and lights. Then she stopped, hand on the key. The porch light was on. By its feeble glow she could see someone sitting on the porch swing. A man.

She waited, staring at the intruder blocking her way to bed. It could be a friend of her neighbor's, waiting for him to come home. Or it could be a mugger. The man rose and moved under the light, then held up a hand in greeting. He walked toward her car.

"Hank." She went to meet him in the warm night. He slid his arms around her and buried his face in her neck.

"Max," he murmured. "My house is too empty. I can't go home. Let me stay here, like I used to. Remember?"

His arms tightened until he had lifted her off the ground. His cheek pressed against hers until the bones of her jaw ached. His fingers dug into her back. She could feel his heart pounding against hers. He gripped her hair and held her mouth against his, his tongue pushing far back into her mouth, his breath filling her.

Stars swirled and danced in dizzying circles through the branches of the maples. The heavy scent of cut grass filled her head. She couldn't breathe. It was like an ocean wave had risen out of a calm sea and knocked her senseless, just like it had been for the brief month they had been lovers.

"It's over, Hank," she gasped. "It was wonderful, but it's over. Stay, tonight. Stay here as long as you want. But not lovers, Hank. That's finished." She forced out the words, remembering the comfort and solice he had brought during the long months after her husband left. Her affair with Hank had been brief and had ended by affectionate mutual consent, neither of them wanting to complicate their lives with anything substantial.

Hank looked down at her, his face in shadow. Then he put his arm around her and started walking toward the house, his steps matching hers, across the porch, up the stairs, across the dark pattern of the Sarouk, and down the darker hall to her bed, where the luminous green of the digital clock guided her toward the pillows.

In the morning, the only way she even knew he had been there was the sheet on the couch, and the prescription form with his scrawl on it. It rested against a single red rose on the kitchen table. "Maxene St. Clair, one or more daily. H. Myer, M.D."

CHAPTER

4

DETECTIVE JOSEPH GRABOWSKI was sitting in the Milwaukee Public Library on Sixth and Wisconsin, waiting for the young librarian to find the information he had asked for. The woman was still reading the columns of microfiche references, something she had been doing off and on for the better part of an hour. In between, she had hunted through volumes almost too heavy for her to carry.

"Only in Milwaukee would I be searching for this in the public library instead of in computerized police files," he said to the young woman. She paused in her scanning of the microfiche and looked up at him, not understanding his sarcasm about the Milwaukee Police Department and its lack of computer files. The pause was only a fraction of a second. The glance at him seemed to energize her, or maybe it was his smile. Or maybe it was her quick peek at his ringless finger.

He watched her pull another plastic sheet from the microfiche book and insert it into the machine. The more false leads she found, the more determined she grew. A real detective. Finally, she came upon a small entry in the microfiche that sent her to an immense volume under the counter. There she found a footnote that sent her scurrying into the reference stacks.

Grabowski watched her disappear into the rows of books and sat down at one of the long tables between the acres of chest-high bookshelves of the general fiction section. Detective fiction covered the wall behind him, eight shelves high. Wheeled ladders waited for any reader brave enough to try a book on the top shelf. Today was too hot for courage.

Grabowski put his feet up on another wooden chair. His search for this obscure bit of chemical information had brought him from the ovenlike fourth floor at the Police Administration Building on Seventh and State, where the ventilation system couldn't handle the ninety-degree heat outside and the five o'clock sun blasting in the windows. He had been writing a rape/homicide report that was grim and boring at the same time. His mind kept sheering off. He had been watching the dust motes in the slanting sun when his lieutenant tossed a business-sized envelope onto his desk.

"Find out what this is all about," he had said. "It could get you into air-conditioned houses, out of this heat."

And it was hot. Milwaukee was roasting in the usual July heat plus 90 percent humidity. Office air conditioners broke down, car radiators boiled over in midtown traffic, bums had heat strokes in front of the State Street missions and died without ever waking from their alcoholic stupors. In the parks, rats invaded overflowing trash cans and scurried out to frighten children. People fanned themselves on shaded porches or under backyard elms, waiting until midnight to venture into stifling bedrooms.

Grabowski's pants legs, damp with sweat, had stuck to the wooden chair. The library wasn't air-conditioned, but then neither were many buildings in Milwaukee. Summer was too short to warrant the expense, and besides, the solidly built buildings withstood the heat unless there was an unbroken stretch of temperatures in the nineties. Even then, evenings were cool enough so that most buildings cooled off.

He unstuck his pants from his skin. The cotton seersucker was already wrinkled, although he had only been working a few hours. Grabowski always looked wrinkled in summer. Fashionable dress wasn't a job requirement.

Grabowski rubbed his face to push away the tiredness. He had been struggling for weeks with a crime wave that seemed more related to heat-triggered tempers than to actual increase in real crime. Homicide cases had outnumbered burglaries for a week—nothing premeditated, just people pushed to the brink by heat and circumstance. He pitied the police officers who were first on the scene and had to face assailants still maddened by the heat.

The scrape of his chair had roused the occupants of his table, three bums the earnest young librarian had referred to as "transients." They stared at him bleary-eyed, then put their heads back down and went to sleep. They had propped books in front of them but had given up all pretense of reading.

"You want me to run them out of here?" he had asked the young librarian when he first came into the library. He had flashed his badge discreetly. She stared at it, startled, then his smile reassured her.

"There aren't many people here now." She smiled, look-ing at the bums with sympathy. "They can stay in out of the heat."

Or cold, or rain, or snow. Bums were a permanent fixture in the downtown library. He knew that from the years he had spent there himself, studying for his BA in political science from Marquette University, a few blocks down Wisconsin Avenue from the library. That was ten years ago. Add the years before that in Vietnam, and he had been an old man by Marquette student standards by the time he worked his way through. Now he was planning to do it all again—only this time to law school.

Or was he? He was beginning to wonder if forty was too old for reeducating. The captain and inspector of detectives had urged him to apply—said they needed a detective who could outwit the lawyers as well as the criminals. They had even promised him three year's leave of absence to go to school full-time, plus his job back at an advanced salary.

The problem was, he wasn't sure now that he wanted to be a lawyer. He didn't like lawyers—at least the fast-talking, money-hungry group he faced across the witness stand every time one of his arrests went to trial. The desire to become an attorney had started as an acute irritation with the ease that slick criminal lawyers were blocking his arrests from reaching convictions. He watched the lawyers in action long enough to spot patterns, then figured out how to plug some of the holes in his cases.

After a while, many of his cases held together long enough to reach conviction. At that point, he noticed that the criminal lawyers taking on his cases were the higher-priced variety—the best that criminal money could buy. It then gave him enormous satisfaction to watch the high-priced lawyers turn into the ambulance chasers, and the graduates straight out of law school who were the only ones desperate enough to take on losing cases. Still, he lost enough to wish he knew more about the legal mental process that was outsmarting him.

"There's a lot these bastards know that I don't," he had muttered once to his captain, pouring another beer down his throat after watching a sure conviction turn into a puff of air. "I should go to law school and find out."

Surprisingly, his captain had nodded. "You're as smart as any of them. You may actually figure out tricks they don't know."

The next afternoon, a note in his box told him to report to the inspector's office. An application to Marquette was lying on the table. The inspector tossed it over.

"We want you to apply," he growled. "The cops in this town have a bad reputation for low IQs. We want a few eggheads around to show the mayor we're not just animals carrying guns."

"You think I can get in?" A wave of power flooded him, surprising him.

"I can't guarantee it, if that's what you're asking. I know a few people there, but we're on opposite sides of the bench."

"I didn't want you to pull strings."

"I would if I could. You're too smart to be happy spending your life chasing drug dealers. I want your brains back in action, keep you from getting bored. We'll pay, of course.

Best investment this department ever made."

"You gonna be one of *them*?" his partner had said pointedly, when Grabowski told him that Marquette had sent the letter of acceptance.

He had smiled. "I'm still going to be me."

But that wasn't certain. Any intensive training changed a person. He had watched it happen in Vietnam. Law school was no less an indoctrination than military. His friends who went to law school behaved differently afterward than they had before; they "processed information" differently, as his anthropology professor would have said. Becoming a lawyer meant acquiring the attitude that your brain was for hire, regardless of a client's guilt or innocence. The attitude was opposite a police officer's. Police enforced written law. Lawyers tried to circumvent, avoid, or even break the law. Grabowski liked being a policeman. When he had applied to law school he had thought he would like knowing the other side of the fence. Now he wasn't sure.

The librarian came back. She had put on pink lipstick and combed her blond curls. She showed him a single small volume, apologizing for the wait, then opened the book and pointed out a paragraph. Not much, she said, but the best she could find. The cool cloth of her shirt brushed his arm. If he would come back, she said, she would look more, but now she had to help other people. Ask at the science library at Marquette, she added, or the chemistry or biology library.

And come back. She handed over the volume slowly. He smiled at her, promising nothing, then photocopied the page and dropped the book into the book return slot. His footsteps echoed on the cool marble floor, down the long, wide, book-lined hall to the marble rotunda entrance. He looked upward, as he always did when he left the library, to see who was pacing the narrow walkway around the second floor of the rotunda. Someone was usually there, thinking out a mental problem while walking the reassuring roundness. Perhaps he should walk that circumference himself.

In the meantime, he had only this small bit of information, the name of an obscure nerve poison, to start the long investigative process—asking questions, more questions, walking from house to house, office to office, until a pattern emerged.

He pushed open the heavy brass-studded doors to Wisconsin Avenue and stood at the top of the stone steps between the giant stone lions resting on their haunches. Below him, the traffic rushed by, buffeting him with heat and noise. His watch said five o'clock. He could grab some fish fries at the bar off State Street near Deaconess Hospital, then drive over to St. Agnes Hospital on Twenty-first and Locust. He could get the case started tonight by interviewing the pathologist who had sent in the blood sample. A phone call to the hospital switchboard had confirmed he was there.

Maxene might be at St. Agnes, too, working in the ER. He cheered up at the prospect of seeing Maxene again. She possessed the physician's skill of listening carefully to what someone said, but she had the added gift of listening beyond the words to what wasn't being said. Maxene had done some type of biochemical research when she was a professor at Marquette, he vaguely remembered her saying once when he had taken her out to dinner. That was all he could remember, though. He had done all the talking.

Maybe she could get a few minutes' break for coffee, or agree to another dinner. He needed to talk to her about law school. She could help him decide whether to go. On the other hand, it was embarrassing to tell someone with her advanced degrees about the dilemma of going back to school. She would automatically advise him to do it. Or maybe she wouldn't, he thought again. Maxene St. Clair wasn't a person who assumed that other people's stories should read the same as hers.

CHAPTER

5

THE ARMED FORCES Institute of Pathology takes its own sweet time about sending pathology reports, at least that's what Aaron Simonson told St. Clair after he mailed off the new blood samples for Nanette Myer's postmortem. So when Simonson phoned Maxene in the emergency room Monday evening after the funeral—only five days after he had mailed off the samples, St. Clair didn't connect the call with Nanette Myer.

Dr. St. Clair was in the process of trying to argue a teenage drug abuser out of a prescription of Tussionex, a codeine cough syrup sold on the street for triple its prescription price. Street users extracted the synthetic codeine by spinning the bottle around their heads on a string until the narcotic separated from the suspension liquid. St. Clair scowled at the anorectic adolescent twitching nervously on the exam table.

"You're getting Robitussin DM," she said shortly, scribbling the prescription on her pad and tossing it onto the exam table. "Same thing without the codeine. And work on your cough; it's still phony."

"Hey, wait," the kid whined, a note of panic in his voice, but St. Clair was gone. She shrugged her shoulders to shake off her anger. Emergency room doctors were favorite marks for drug dealers, but she could never develop the indifference of other ER staff. She always felt the urge to call the narcotics squad and have the patient dragged off.

Joella was waving a pink telephone message slip. "Dr. Simonson wants you in the Path lab," she called. "Stat."

St. Clair fled.

Aaron Simonson was waiting in his quiet lab that was chokingly redolent of formaldehyde and decaying tissue. He was sitting across his desk from another man who had his back to the door. Simonson's fleshy lips seemed paler than usual, and his normally colorless complexion had bleached further to cadaver gray.

"Someone called the cops," he said as St. Clair pushed open the swinging doors.

The man facing him turned, and the surprise on his face made St. Clair smile.

"Grabowski! But shouldn't you be waiting for stitches in the ER?"

"I wish I were," he replied, no trace of smile. "You were the last person I wanted to see come through that door."

Confusion dampened St. Clair's pleasure at seeing Grabowski again. The last time they met was across a candlelit table. He had taken her to a south side Yugoslavian restaurant—white tablecloths, strolling violinists. They had talked until the place closed. Grabowski had been good company. He looked like the typical Polish cop she sewed up in the ER—lots of dark hair, an untidy mustache, muscled, and slightly rumpled. He was thinner than the usual cop but wore the traditional bland expression. He was also different in that at forty he was married only to his work.

Dinner had been an oasis for her in a week of car accidents and muggings. Then St. Clair was working when Grabowski was off, and vice versa, for weeks.

"Is this business?" she asked. "I don't see any blood."

Simonson answered for him. "It seems the AFIP sent a copy of Nanette Myer's pathology results to the police, instead of sending them here. Nosy bastards, aren't they?"

Grabowski interrupted. "Someone wondered why a fatal dose of," he consulted a paper in his hand, "tetrodotoxin, was found in a blood sample sent in by a hospital lab. They were suspicious enough to give us a call."

St. Clair's stomach lurched. She felt lightheaded. "Tetrodotoxin?" she heard her voice quaver.

"It was an obscure enough poison that they even used the word murder," Grabowski said.

The fluorescent lights of the lab danced in front of St. Clair's eyes. The room spun, and an uncertain darkness closed around her. When the darkness retreated to the edge of the picture, St. Clair was stretched out on the autopsy table, Grabowski was fanning her with the police report, and Simonson was taking her pulse. St. Clair twitched her wrist away. Simonson's clammy fingers weren't anywhere near her pulse. The pathologist hadn't touched a live patient in years and wouldn't know a pulse if he found one. St. Clair sat up.

Simonson poured himself a cup of coffee. He started to take a sip, then handed it to her. "Your guess about the tetrodotoxin was right," he said. "There was enough toxin in that sample to knock off a dinner party."

St. Clair slid off the autopsy table, the thought of joining the previous occupants bringing her out of her faint with a jolt. The world still wobbled, though, and she let Grabowski guide her to a chair.

"Since when does a case-hardened emergency room doctor faint at the news of violent death?" Grabowski demanded.

"I wasn't expecting it. And I missed dinner."

Grabowski looked at her for a long moment with no expression on his face. Finally he said, "Dr. Simonson says you were the person who suggested testing for tetrodotoxin. What made you think of that poison?"

"The symptoms. I was talking over the case with a colleague from Marquette, and he pointed out that those were the symptoms of a neurotoxin. Nerve poison, in layman's terms."

"I've never heard of tetrodotoxin."

"Neither have most people around here, but about four hundred people in Japan were poisoned by it in the last two years. Over half died."

Grabowski was scribbling notes; Simonson looking carefully away. Maxene plunged ahead recklessly.

"The poison comes from the puffer fish, a spiny ugly tropical fish that frightens off predators by puffing itself up to many times its normal size. The fish is delicious, I'm told, but if you accidentally eat the ovaries, you may have eaten your last meal. The fish is also found in shallow waters off Hawaii, Australia, and South Africa. As a murder weapon, it isn't new. I've seen it used on TV detective shows."

Grabowski looked startled. "How do you know so much about this deadly stuff?"

St. Clair drew a breath. The bad news had to be faced sooner or later. "I used it when I was doing research at Marquette and teaching at the Medical College of Wisconsin. I kept vials of it in the desk drawer of my lab." Nausea flooded her, although that could have been the coffee.

Grabowski's expression changed from interested to cautious. "Let's start again, at the beginning. How long ago did you use the poison?"

"I started about three years ago, and finished six months ago."

"Anyone else use it?"

"My research assistant, Nathan Schalz. He handled it under my supervision. No one else in Milwaukee, or even in Wisconsin, is using it, that I know. There's an M.D. Ph.D. in Atlanta who's doing similar research to mine, and he uses tetrodotoxin as part of his experiments. Both of us were trying to determine the effects of chemicals on the metabolism of digoxin on the heart. The researcher in Atlanta felt that tetrodotoxin didn't affect digoxin. I thought it had an effect, but that it wore off because it was reacting with chemicals in the chemical bath where the heart muscle sat during experiments. The chemicals deactivated it."

Grabowski held up a hand. "Skip the research for the moment. What you're saying is that this person from Georgia is the only one you know who had legitimate access to tetrodotoxin, besides you."

"You could check with the Micro Ellen Chemical Company in New York. They sell the drug to researchers. But anyone who works in exotic seafood restaurants can get puffer fish ovaries. Or people who travel to Japan, Hawaii, Australia, or South Africa could bring the poison back in its raw form, if they want to carry fish ovaries in their suitcases."

Grabowski was writing. "Who else knew you had this poison?"

"I prefer to think of it as a research drug, if you don't mind."

"Suit yourself. Who knew?"

"My research wasn't secret. Anyone could come into my lab to watch my research methods, and lots of students did. Besides that, I was funded by a drug company and a university research grant, and I had to submit detailed reports to both every year. The drug company may have kept my reports confidential, but the medical college keeps those in faculty files and in the research grant files. Anyone who gets by the secretary can read them. I also had to give talks at university alumni functions to prove to alumni that the university had live researchers on the premises. In fact, that's how I met Nanette Myer—at a Board of Regents dinner. Her husband is on the board."

The blare from the hospital paging system made them all jump. "Dr. St. Clair to the ER."

"I'm wanted, sorry. You can finish interrogating me later." She pushed out the double doors, fighting the urge to run.

The onslaught of sick and wounded kept St. Clair busy until after eleven. She finished taping an IV line to the arm of a gunshot victim—above the handcuff—and called an orderly to wheel him to surgery, accompanied by an armed policeman.

"Keep an eye on the cop," St. Clair murmured to the orderly. "I don't want any more holes in this patient until surgery."

The orderly rolled his eyes.

After they left, St. Clair dropped into her favorite red plastic armchair in the supply room and put up her feet.

Her first hypothesis had proven correct. Nanette Myer was poisoned and by tetrodotoxin. But was it murder? Couldn't it have been pure accident?

Pick another hypothesis, she told herself. Get a starting point, then line up the facts as they come in and let the facts prove or disprove your hypothesis. She grabbed a hospital memo pad from the shelf and wrote across the top, Hypothesis: Nanette Myer was deliberately poisoned by tetrodotoxin. The harsh black and white words had an energizing effect, order on chaos. Now she had to gather data. St. Clair felt the small jolt of excitement that she always felt at the beginning of a new research project. She continued writing. One: Determine where the tetrodotoxin came from. Restaurant, unknown traveler, my lab.

No conclusions yet, she warned herself. She shoved the memo pad into her pocket and went out to the nurse's station to telephone her old research assistant at Marquette.

The nurse's station was quiet. Joella was smoking in the bathroom, according to a note taped to the phone, and Shirley was cleaning up the aftermath of the gunshot victim. St. Clair dialed her old number at the university biochemistry building. Even though it was eleven at night, it was most likely that Nathan was there.

Nathan Schalz was a Ph.D. candidate in immunology who supported himself as a research assistant for anyone with funds to hire him. He had worked for Dr. St. Clair for four years while he did his own research, sharing her lab, an arrangement more intimate than marriage. Schalz kept the hours of a typical researcher, working around the clock when test results were coming in, hibernating when exhaustion hit. St. Clair's ex-husband had worked the same schedule, even sleeping on a cot in his office when results were coming off the computer or out of a test tube. At least he had slept there until the night St. Clair dropped in and found the cot occupied by two.

The phone rang thirteen times. Someone lifted the receiver, but no voice answered.

"Nathan," St. Clair spoke clearly. "Are you awake?"

No answer.

"Nathan, this is Maxene St. Clair. Please speak."

"Umm?"

"Nathan, I have to talk to you. Tonight. Name a time."

Schalz was a meticulous researcher, obsessed with detail. When he was awake. Asleep, he was a pathology case.

"One o'clock," he groaned. "Lab. Data coming off the computer." The phone clattered to the floor.

Shirley was leaning her elbows on the counter.

"This have anything to do with the Myer murder case?"

"Who says it's murder?"

"Got to be murder when that good-looking detective you go out with starts hanging around here asking questions. Lucky you're in good with him or you'd already be arrested."

"Don't be silly."

"Honey, you knew the dead woman, you used the poison in your research, and you were in charge when she died. I hear you're real friendly with the husband, too."

St. Clair felt her face break out in a sweat. Had anyone found out about her affair with Hank Myer? Not that she wasn't willing to be held accountable for her actions. But now that the police thought Nanette Myer might have been murdered, letting Hank Myer spend the night at her flat only twelve hours after the funeral took on a new and horrible meaning.

"Is there no limit to rumor in this hospital?" she snapped. "I knew the husband because we are both doctors and we work in the same hospital."

"And you go to parties at his house."

"So do a lot of people."

"Not me." Shirley picked up a blank chart and went off to greet the next patient.

By 12:30 A.M., Dr. St. Clair finished charting and walked to the doctor's parking lot accompanied by the security guard. The temperature was simmering in the humid low eighties, and the stars were an obscure glimmer beyond the lights and haze of the city. The stars would be brighter at her apartment on the east side, and it would be cooler, from the soft summer breeze off Lake Michigan. She thought with longing of the dark bed waiting for her. But she hardened her resolve. Nanette Myer may have died of tetrodotoxin from her lab. Maxene had to find out. Better her than the police. She could figure out how it happened before they started alarming everyone with their questions. Besides, she was fresh off nine hours of giving orders; she was still in the take-charge mood.

She turned her car south toward the Marquette campus on Wisconsin Avenue where her old lab assistant would be hard at work.

The campus buildings were dark and quiet, disturbed only by the sporadic rush of downtown traffic that ringed the campus and the faint whisper of the breeze-rustled ivy that crawled over the brick and stone buildings. St. Clair drove through the unguarded gates and parked on the sidewalk by the carved wooden doors of the biochemistry building. She tried not to look at the dark recesses between the adjoining buildings.

A wino was sleeping in the cool stone portico at the front door, his filthy toes pointing at the sky through the holes in his shoes. St. Clair reached cautiously over his body—who knew when a wino would relieve himself—and pushed her key into the door, grateful she had forgotten to return her keys when she left the university. She wrenched open the door and slipped into the dark building, groping toward the banister to guide her up the steps. Moving quietly, in case a mugger was lurking inside, she crept up the worn stone steps to the third floor. A trek through Nepal would have seemed shorter.

A line of light under Nathan's lab door guided her down the last hallway. She breathed a sigh of relief and pushed open the door into the brightly lit room. Then she stopped short.

Detective Joseph Grabowski was lounging against the computer.

"What are you doing here?" she snapped.

"Mr. Schalz told me you were coming, when I called earlier. I decided to come, too, and find out what was so urgent."

"Nothing is urgent. I wanted to find out if the tetrodotoxin came from my lab—the same reason you're here."

Schalz looked relieved. "Detective, uh, Grabowski, was asking about your research, and I told him my part of it. But you should talk about your own research, don't you think? Go right ahead while I have dinner. Want some?" He dragged a limp and shriveled bologna and cheese sandwich out of a wrinkled brown sack.

St. Clair regarded him coldly. "No. And stop babbling like I have something to conceal."

Grabowski had flipped open his notebook and was scanning a page. "I spent the evening calling up every restaurant in town to find who serves puffer fish," he began. "So far no one does. The airlines have given us lists of people on their flights to those countries where people can get puffer fish ovaries, and we're going through those names now. But the fact is, the only sure source of tetrodotoxin we have is this lab."

St. Clair sat down at her old desk in the corner and put her feet up on the cold radiator. It was nice to be back. How many times had she sat just like this, waiting for something to happen inside a computer, waiting for something to happen inside a beaker? How many years had she spent just waiting?

"Maxene," Grabowski interrupted her musing. "According to you and Mr. Schalz, you got your tetrodotoxin from a chemical supply house. They sent the appropriate amounts, and you stored them in your desk."

St. Clair nodded. Grabowski turned to Schalz. "You helped Dr. St. Clair with her experiments, and you had ready access to all the toxin for three years."

"Two and a half. Max left here six months ago."

"But you had access."

"Sure. The only time I couldn't get the stuff was when Max locked her desk, but she rarely did that. Max forgets to lock anything. I bet her car's unlocked right now and so is her apartment."

St. Clair winced. Both times she had dinner with Grabowski, they had returned to find her front door unlocked. Once it was actually standing open. Grabowski had insisted upon searching the place, an event that had delayed his departure, agreeably.

"Tell me more about this tetrodotoxin," Grabowski said. "What does it do?"

St. Clair drew a breath. "Without getting too technical, tetrodotoxin is a popular research chemical because it paralyzes live heart muscle without killing it, so to speak. Heart muscle can be kept functional for a few days by suspending it in a chemical bath similar to body fluid. Then experiments can be done on the heart. For example, I wanted to see how digitalis acted on heart muscle. One theory says digitalis works because it's actively pumped by a chemical process across the cell membrane. Tetrodotoxin paralyzes the pump. Our procedure was to put a guinea pig's heart on a strain gauge in a liquid bath that resembled body fluid. Then we attached the heart to a machine that electrically stimulated it to beat at a certain rate."

"Skip the details," said Grabowski, looking nauseated. "What does this tetrodotoxin look like? Does it have a smell or a taste?"

"It came as a clear liquid in glass vials that were one cubic centimeter in size. I never noticed an odor, but the stink in this lab might have blocked that. As far as taste, I hope never to find out."

"Did you just pour it over the heart?"

"Certainly not. Tetrodotoxin is powerful and shockingly expensive. I got ten vials at a time from the chemical supply house. I would break open one vial at a time and make a ten percent solution by mixing one cc of tetrodotoxin with nine cc's of distilled water. I diluted that further with chemical bath into five graduated solutions that ranged from point oh one percent to two percent. I used them in the experiment, then at the end of the day I poured it down the sink."

"Did you ever have any of the ten percent solution left over?"

"Sometimes."

"Where did you keep that? In your drawer with the vials?"

"No. In the lunchroom refrigerator." St. Clair ducked mentally, expecting an outburst. She got it.

"You kept a deadly poison in a lunchroom refrigerator? Someone might have drunk it! Or spilled it in their food!" Grabowski's voice rose with his eyebrows. "I'm surprised no one died before now!"

"The flask was stoppered with a tight cork and carefully labeled. No one could get into it accidentally. Everyone who has chemicals that need refrigeration keeps them in the lunchroom refrigerator."

"That's right." Nathan came to her support. "This is an old building, and we don't have good storage facilities. Our department head asked for a lab refrigerator in her last grant proposal, but so far the NIH hasn't come through."

"Someone could have stolen the bottle out of the refrigerator."

"The refrigerator is locked. Keys are issued by the janitor."

Grabowski raised an eyebrow and jotted a few notes. "Who's your department head?" he demanded.

"Dr. Virginia Gaust. Her office is down the hall. She uses this lab for her research, too. When Maxene worked here, we all shared it."

"Show me the lunchroom."

Nathan led the way down the dark hall to the first door by the stairs.

"Not locked, I see," Grabowski observed, pushing open the door. He turned on the wall switch and opened the refrigerator. "Also unlocked. Anyone could steal anything."

Nathan glanced guiltily at St. Clair. "Everyone's careless about locking up. But we've never had anything stolen, except food."

"How would you know?" Grabowski demanded. He threw up his hands in exasperation. "Someone could have poured some out. You'd never miss a few cc's."

"Yes, we would," Schalz said promptly. "I recorded every cc as we used it. When one flask was empty, I added up my recorded cc's to make sure they totaled what we started with. They always did."

"Someone could have replaced a few cc's with water. Like filling up a whiskey bottle with water so it looks like you didn't drink any. Would an experiment not work out if you were using additionally diluted toxin?"

St. Clair exchanged glances with Schalz. "Good point," she admitted. "I could review my lab data to see if there were periods where results were off. Maybe a pattern would emerge. But results can vary for lots of reasons. The concentration of the bath the heart muscle sits in changes the reaction time. Or the temperature of the room makes a difference. Sometimes, whenever the lab air conditioner goes out, this room turns into an oven. The temperature of the bath goes up and raises the reaction time. Also, the hot room increases evaporation in the bath, and that strengthens the concentration."

Nathan added, "Besides that, a fresh heart muscle reacts more quickly than one that's even a few minutes old. If it took Maxene longer than three minutes to kill the guinea pig, dissect out the heart, and cut out a piece of the atrium, there would be damage to the heart muscle, and it would react less well."

Grabowski stared at St. Clair. "You actually killed guinea pigs and cut out their hearts? And you timed how long it took?"

"How else do you think we got fresh heart muscle?" Maxene snapped. "Ordered it from the supermarket, like chicken liver?"

"How many of these little pets died for your experiments?" Grabowski persisted.

St. Clair gritted her teeth. "Let's not get into that, shall we? Laboratory medicine has to sacrifice animals."

"Tell that to the jury. The prosecuting attorney will have a field day when he starts describing how you routinely murdered helpless animals. A jury won't take an hour to convict you of murdering that woman."

St. Clair clutched her hair. "Grabowski, I did not murder that woman. Murdering guinea pigs, I mean sacrificing guinea pigs, is not the same as murdering humans."

Grabowski was scribbling notes. "What happened to all your toxin when you quit doing research?"

Schalz answered. "We had two vials left, plus part of a flask of diluted solution. I totaled up the cc's in the flask to make sure we had the right amount left, then we poured the diluted solution down the sink and packed up the other two vials to mail back to the chemical supply house. We took the package to the post office and went for pizza and beer with the pharmacology and immunology departments."

"Does the EPA know you pour chemical toxins into the sewers?"

Nathan winced. "We stopped. It's considered toxic waste now."

They walked down the dark hall and into the lab. "You still have your records?" Grabowski asked Nathan.

"Of course. You never know what slip of paper might lead to a Nobel Prize." He rummaged through his filing cabinet and handed over two thick folders. "Don't lose anything. You could set science back ten years."

Grabowski flipped through the pages covered with neat columns of numbers. St. Clair peered over his shoulder. The familiar data sheets gave her a curious homesick feeling, plus boredom. Did she really want to come back to this?

"You have similar folders?" Grabowski asked her.

"Evidence, you mean?" she said, coldly. "At my apartment."

She walked out of the building with Grabowski, following the click of his footsteps on the black stairs. Her fingers itched to take his arm in the dark, but she resisted. Murder suspects shouldn't be leaning on police. Instead, she fell over his heels when he stopped in the pool of darkness at the bottom of the steps. She grabbed at the back of his jacket. The ridges of seersucker felt reassuring and familiar.

The wino was still snoring heavily in the stone portico. Grabowski took her elbow politely as she stepped over the reeking body, then he opened the unlocked door of her car and peered into the backseat.

"Unlocked again," he accused, slamming the door. "One day a mugger will hide in your backseat and throttle you for your loose change."

"I've heard the lecture before from hospital security." She reached for the door handle, but Grabowski intercepted her hand and held it, leaning against the car.

"Answer a few questions," he demanded, quietly. "First, this is a very nice place to work. Quaint little lab, interesting research, helpful lab assistant, even if he looks like a troll. Why did you leave?"

St. Clair groaned. "I told you before, remember? Over a glass of wine."

"Tell me again."

"It's a sordid tale of mismatched marriage and thwarted ambition—one I'm trying to forget. I was an assistant professor here, with a small academic salary and some respectable research grants. After about six years, I met and married another assistant professor who also had a research grant. The marriage lasted two years—as long as his grant. There were conflicts, like domestic incompatibility, infidelity on his part, and the fact that my research got refunded and his didn't. He left for the University of Iowa with a nubile chemistry student. After my divorce, my research didn't seem relevant, to use a term from the sixties. So I took a year's leave of absence and went to work at St. Agnes emergency room to figure out what to do with my life. My leave will be up in six months, and I'll come back. Maybe."

"So your divorce soured you on research. You didn't leave for other reasons."

Maxene removed her hand from his. "I didn't leave so I could kill Hank Myer's wife with poison that might not be traced to me any longer."

"Stop being flippant, Maxene." Grabowski gripped her arms. "You've got your ass in a sling, and you better think how to get it out."

"You're hurting me, Grabowski. What do you mean my ass is in a sling? I knew Nanette slightly, and the poison may have come from my lab, but that doesn't connect me to her."

"She died under your care, Max. The prosecutor will say you avoided treatment that could have saved her."

"I didn't know she had neurotoxin poisoning when she came in. I thought she had heart failure, which is what I treated her for. Even the autopsy showed heart failure. Besides, I arranged for the additional postmortem blood tests. I could have left the diagnosis as heart failure."

"The prosecutor will say you were worried that someone else would decide heart failure was an unusual finding for such a young woman, and you wanted to make yourself look good." Grabowski rubbed his forehead. "Max, I like you very much, but I've been assigned to this case, and I have to find out who killed that woman."

"I am equally eager to find that out, Detective Grabowski," St. Clair said coldly. "I feel very badly about this woman's death and my association with the poison that killed her. For my own peace of mind, I would like to make sure that the poison didn't come from my lab. But if it did—if I had a lapse of technique that allowed some toxin to slip away from me—any investigation will show I didn't kill her. I barely knew her."

Grabowski sighed. The faint glow of the streetlight caught the sag of his shoulders. "I've spent the last five hours tracing the movements of anyone closely associated with Nanette Myer. One unfortunate fact I dug up is that Hank Myer got a parking ticket about fifteen hours after his wife was buried. The address on the ticket was on your block, Max. He got a citation at two A.M. when the street sweeper reported his car was parked on the wrong side of the street. It looks like Dr. Myer spent the night at your apartment, not twelve hours after he buried his wife. That has to be the most incriminating piece of evidence I ever saw—for him or for you!"

St. Clair felt dismay pour through her like a hail shower. "That had nothing to do with his wife's death," she protested. "The night Hank came over, I didn't even know Nanette had been poisoned. I thought she died of heart failure."

"Even if that were true, how could you sleep with a man the very day he buried his wife?"

St. Clair felt her face flush. "He was all alone and needed company. I had to invite him inside. I admit the impropriety."

"Did you have to make love?"

St. Clair felt anger build under humiliation. "Are you so upset because sex with Hank Myer incriminates me somehow or because you're jealous? And how do you know I slept with him? Do you have spies in the bedroom?"

"You haven't denied it."

"Well, damn you to hell." She slammed the door and gunned the car off the sidewalk. In the rearview mirror, she could see him standing alone under the faint and receding glow of the streetlight.

CHAPTER

6

BY 10:00 THE next morning, Joseph Grabowski was wishing he were back in the inner city interrogating car thieves. He had watched with mixed emotions as Maxene drove off the night before. Predominant was fury—at her and at himself. How could she be so stupid as to sleep with the husband of a murdered woman? And why was Grabowski letting himself care? He really should take himself off the case, he decided.

He had gone home and spent several sleepless hours sitting on the front porch of his bungalow on Milwaukee's south side, watching the faint fluorescence of Lake Michigan on the other side of the street glow against the beach. How had he gotten into such an emotional state? The shock of discovering that Maxene knew everything there was to know about the poison that killed Nanette Myer was doubled by the horror of learning she was having an affair with the murdered woman's husband.

He had gone to bed for a few restless hours, then was up by 8:00. The people involved in this case were day people, not night people like his usual burglary, robbery, arson, and rape cases. He had to shift his hours to daylight.

At 9:00 A.M. he arrived at Hank Myer's office at the appointed time. A silent receptionist motioned him to a chair in the waiting room. He looked at the pharmaceutical representative and the octogenarians already waiting and sighed. Half an hour later he was still cooling his heels and his sweat-damp clothing in the cold blast of the air conditioner. The frigid air raised goose bumps on Grabowski's arms in his short-sleeved shirt and sent cold shocks down his back.

At 10:00, Myer finally beckoned to him from the doorway. He was wearing a beige silk-weave jacket with a subdued lavender tie, and he looked elegantly comfortable. Grabowski followed Myer down a short hallway graced with watercolor sketches of flowers and into a book-lined office.

Myer dropped casually into a leather chair behind a vast mahogany desk and waved Grabowski to a smaller version. The white carpet, white floor-length drapes, and large oriental rug deadened sound. Grabowski felt like he was in a tomb. The tomb effect was heightened by an antiseptic clinic smell. Grabowski looked at the Erte prints on the wall and made a mental note to find out Myer's net worth and how much he would inherit from his wife's estate. He also mentally compared the office to Maxene's theater of operations at the ER. He wondered if Maxene would ever progress to this type of medical clinic. On the other hand, was this progress?

An hour was too long to wait at this early hour of the morning, Grabowski had long since decided. His patience was worn thin.

"We've come upon evidence that your wife didn't die of heart failure," Grabowski began, curtly. "We received a report from the Armed Forces Institute of Pathology that she somehow consumed a significant quantity of a poison which killed her."

Myer's eyes widened. "Poison?"

"It's called tetrodotoxin. It's an obscure poison that comes from a fish."

Myer rubbed his lips. "Poison?"

Grabowski continued, telling him the natural origin of the toxin and how it had been discovered in his wife's blood.

"A fish!" Myer said finally, his voice hoarse. "Nanette didn't like fish, even in glass tanks."

"Can you tell me if your wife ate any fish the day she died? In a restaurant, at someone's home? Maybe she bought some from a fish market?"

"I doubt it. She didn't eat fish if she could help it. But I don't know what she did that day. I didn't see her. I know that sounds strange for two people to live together and not even see each other, and I feel bad about it. With my schedule, though, it happened a lot. That morning I had seven o'clock surgery at Deaconess Hospital, then I went straight from there to the Amtrak Station. I was supposed to appear on a panel at a two-day conference at the downtown Sheraton in Chicago. I caught the eight-thirty commuter train and got to the Sheraton just in time to give my talk. I was at the conference all day, then after dinner I went up to my room, which is where I was when my nurse called to say Nanette had died."

"Do you have any idea what your wife did all day?"

"I assume she went to class at Marquette. She was getting her masters in fine arts."

"How do you feel about that, Dr. Myer?"

"Feel?" Myer frowned. "I wasn't sure what she planned to do with a master's, but I thought if she wanted to do it, I was happy to pay. Nanette was thirty-five. Old enough to know what she wanted."

"Could you give me the names of people she might have seen that day, might have had lunch with?"

Myer shook his head. "If they were art students from Marquette, I wouldn't know their names. She didn't bring any students home. You could ask her professors, or talk to the tennis pro at the Spring Lawn Tennis Club. That's where she spent her time when she wasn't in class. The pro could tell you who she was playing tennis with."

Grabowski wrote down the name of the pro.

"Your wife had a number of medicines in her purse when she came to the ER," he said, consulting his notebook. "Valium, tetracycline, Elavil, Vitamin B Complex. I notice that your name is written on several of the containers as the prescribing physician. Isn't that a little unusual?"

Myer shrugged. "Not really. Most of them were refills from an exam by her own doctor. It was easier for me to write a prescription than for her to call her doctor."

"Why was she taking them?"

"The tranquilizers were for nerves. She had developed a small dependency on them, but nothing dangerous. The tetracycline was for a minor chest cold. She insisted on an antibiotic. The Vitamin B did her more good."

"Have you been to Hawaii, Japan, or Australia recently?" Grabowski continued. It was a foolish way to find out if a husband had brought back poison to kill his wife, he knew, but Myer had sat with so little expression on his face during the interview, Grabowski decided to see how far he could push.

Myer didn't seem to notice the inference. He shook his head. "We went to the Bahamas every January, and last April we went to Paris, but we haven't gone anywhere since."

"What about friends of yours? Have they traveled to any of those places?"

The penny dropped. Myer frowned. "What are you driving at?"

"Someone might have brought back some of the poison and put it into her food or drink."

"You're telling me she was murdered?" The color washed out of his face.

"It's possible."

"With a fish? You're out of your mind!"

"There is one other possibility. The toxin was being used in a research laboratory at Marquette. The poison could have come from there."

"Which research laboratory?"

"Dr. Maxene St. Clair's."

Myer's jaw dropped. "Maxene? Impossible."

"I'm not saying Dr. St. Clair had anything to do with the poisoning. I'm only saying the poison may have come from there."

But Myer's face had closed. He looked at his watch and stood up. "We'll have to continue this another time."

"Dr. Myer, I have other questions, if you don't mind. Why was your wife dressed in such extreme clothing?"

"Extreme? What do you mean?"

"The leather miniskirt, the tight sweater. Was she going to a costume party, perhaps?"

"Nanette was wearing a leather miniskirt the night she died?"

"Yes, sir. And a red wig. Can you tell me why she was wearing them?"

But Myer had already flung open the office door and was hurrying down the hall. The white-capped nurse showed Grabowski out.

The next two hours were equally fruitless. From his car phone, Grabowski had a short and uninformative chat with the doctor whose name was on the Elavil pills container. He hung up after saying a court order to release the files probably wouldn't be necessary. Then he drove out to the tennis club to get the names of the women in Nanette's round-robin tournament. The pro was a muscular man in his early twenties, suitably shocked at the violence of Nanette's death. He could think of no reason why anyone would poison her. Grabowski drew him away from the curious receptionist.

"I hear Mrs. Myer's marriage wasn't entirely happy," he said. "I hear she used to look for happiness in other places." An occasional lie produced an occasional truth.

The pro flushed. "I wouldn't know anything about Mrs. Myer's personal life. If she was, uh, looking for happiness, she was pretty discreet about it. Give me a break, man, why should I start anything with her? I'd lose my job, and she'd mess up her marriage. Have you seen her house? A palace. Maids, gardeners. Who'd chance losing that?"

Grabowski spent the rest of the morning interviewing the women in the round-robin tournament. They were all clones of one another: doctors' wives with tanned, muscular arms and legs, wearing identical knit shirts and cotton print skirts. The interviews took place in air-conditioned splendor, and he downed gallons of mint iced tea, but the answers he got were as inconclusive and frustrating as answers from any hardened criminal. No one knew what Nanette did when she wasn't in medical auxiliary meetings, tennis matches, or art classes at Marquette. No one would speculate as to why she was wearing a black leather miniskirt or a red wig. No one had ever seen that clothing before, even at a Halloween party.

At noon, he finished the final interview. The last house was white stucco with a red-tile roof and black wrought-iron grillwork over the doors and windows. A house built to withstand burglars. Birds fluttered through the water that splashed in the blue-tile fountain in the courtyard. A Doberman answered the doorbell and lifted a lip at him through the glass. The maid took his name through an intercom and led away the dog.

Grabowski mopped the sweat off his neck and hoped this wouldn't be another wasted half hour of endless unanswered questions. He knew by now that Nanette Myer played tennis three days a week and bridge one evening a week. She donated money to lots of charities but took an active interest in none. She had been married twice, the first time before she came to Milwaukee, but no one knew anything about her first husband. Her marriage to Dr. Myer had lasted nine years, no children. Nanette had been a model when they were married and had continued that work off and on until she was thirty-four, when she had gone back to Marquette to get her master's. She occasionally modeled for charity fashion shows.

The interview gave him nothing new. The woman politely allowed him to use the scented guest bathroom to take care of the iced tea he had consumed. She waited quietly in the hall to let him out the front door. The Doberman stood behind her, just as quietly.

Back in the hot car, Grabowski savagely jammed in the clutch. Dead end. If spousal infidelity was part of this murder, the famed medical conspiracy of silence was extending beyond malpractice suits to include it. On the other hand, Nanette Myer might have been killed by someone she knew at Marquette, a professor or a student. This meant Grabowski would have to go back to the Marquette campus again—twice in two days, Grabowski realized. The thought intrigued him; Grabowski didn't believe in coincidence. Besides, interviewing professors and students would give him a chance to look over Marquette again for his own purposes. Maybe the contact would help him decide if he wanted to spend three years sitting in their law library.

The initial hot blast from his car air conditioner nearly took his breath away. He glanced back at the house through his rearview mirror. Through the iron gates of the courtyard he could see the Doberman inside the glass front door, sitting cool and alert on the red-tile floor.

CHAPTER

7

MAXENE ST. CLAIR was rinsing shampoo out of her hair and rehearsing how she would explain to Grabowski that having Hank Myer spend the night at her apartment right after he buried his wife was not a collapse of morals but merely a lapse in judgment, when the doorbell's buzz yanked her out of her teeth gnashing.

Grabowski? At 11:00 A.M.? Normally, he was asleep at this hour. She flung a robe around her wet body and dripped to the top of the stairs. The police officer standing outside the glass front door was wearing a skirt. St. Clair flung open the door with ill grace and stomped back to the bedroom. While she dressed, she could hear drawers in the kitchen and dining room opening and closing.

"If you're searching my apartment, find my yellow can opener," she shouted. When she emerged from the bedroom, the can opener was on the kitchen table.

"What do you want?" St. Clair demanded irritably, running water into the coffee maker. "Whatever your name is."

"Sergeant Lemie. Detective Grabowski sent me to pick up your research files. We don't have a court order so you can refuse, but Detective Grabowski was sure you would cooperate."

"Why didn't he come himself? Still sleeping?"

"He's working on another part of the case. Did you want to talk to him?"

"No." St. Clair wondered how much this attractive young woman knew about her lapse in judgment. She pointed at the two Miller beer boxes filled with papers that sat in the middle of the kitchen floor. She had spent two hours going through them earlier that morning. She found no unusual patterns. Results varied but not greatly. There was no way she could determine if diluted toxin had altered test results.

"Don't lose anything," she snapped at the police woman. "I'll need all that in six months when I go back to the university. Tell that to your detective."

Sergeant Lemie found her way out.

By then it was close to noon. St. Clair ate a carton of yogurt and drove downtown to the university. She needed to talk to someone about this whole mess. Stan Litwack would be good, but Virginia Gaust would be better. Virginia was a top-notch researcher with an analytical mind and an unequaled memory for detail. Virginia might come up with some theory about how the toxin got out of her lab refrigerator and into Nanette Myer—if indeed the poison had come from the lab.

The sweet morning air was thickening to a heavier substance that smelled like brewery yeast. Ozone was materializing into visibility between the downtown office buildings. A gray haze floated over the industrial valley that lay south of the Marquette campus. Beyond the haze stretched the Polish side of Milwaukee, separated from the German north side by the Menominee River, acres of smoky factories, and centuries of hostilities.

St. Clair parked in the parking lot called "Atlantis," because in spring it was under water, and hurried across the now crowded campus to the ivy-covered building she had left only hours before. Inside the building, the chemical aroma overpowered the scent of brewery. Dr. Gaust was sitting at her desk, rifling through computer data sheets.

"Maxene!" she called out with her usual cheerful exuberance. She shoved the data sheets into a drawer. "You're here! And I just got through chatting about you with that cute Polish detective. He says you were right! Nanette didn't die of heart failure! But what's this about your knowing to test for the poison that killed her?"

"Educated guess." St. Clair shifted a stack of exam papers off a chair and sat down. The force of Virginia's curiosity overpowered her, as usual.

"That's like saying you found the needle in the haystack by educated guess. You must have had some reason for testing for that poison. What did you hear? Did this have anything to do with her being dressed up like a hooker?" Virginia was leaning forward, eyes gleaming.

"Stop salivating, Virginia. She was poisoned by the stuff I did research with. I recognized the symptoms of neurotoxin poisoning, that's all. And I don't have any idea why she was dressed like a hooker."

"But you must have known something that tipped you off," Virginia persisted. "When I talked to you at the funeral, you were operating on the hunch that she didn't die of heart failure. Next thing I know, you've put your finger right on the poison."

"Just by the symptoms, Virginia. What did the detective want to know?"

"He asked if anyone could get into your desk besides you. I said that only you had a key. Oh dear, I hope I didn't get you into trouble."

"I managed that by myself. What else did he want to know?"

"How long I'd known you, what kind of researcher you were, how careful you were with your lab chemicals. What's going on, Max?"

Maxene debated how much to tell. Feeding Virginia partial information was worse than telling all. Virginia was apt to fill in the blanks with her imagination and spread it as gospel—an amazing tendency for a research physician. Maxene decided to tell all, except for Hank's appearance in her bedroom during Maxene's divorce, and his overnight stay in her apartment the night after the funeral. Virginia could find that out by herself.

Virginia was mulling it all over when a slovenly figure stopped to slouch in the doorway. Nathan's frizzy hair haloed his head. He draped himself over a chair. Virginia scowled.

"Fill me in," Nathan demanded, pulling a tired pack of vending-machine crackers from his shirt pocket. "Does your detective have his eye on anyone but us? I thought for a minute last night that he was going to finish interrogating us in jail. What else did he say when he walked you to your car?"

Maxene noticed that Virginia was listening with parted lips. "Nothing much," she muttered. "He hasn't found any other source for tetrodotoxin except this lab."

"Maxene!" Virginia gasped theatrically. "If he decides the toxin came from here, where does that leave you?"

"With my ass in a sling, as Grabowski mentioned last night. It also means I'm going to find out who stole it."

"A detective!" Virginia smiled happily. "And I thought the summer was going to be a bore."

Nathan opened another packet of vending-machine crackers and tossed the wrapper toward the wastebasket. He missed. "There are at least twenty people on this floor alone who keep their lunch in that refrigerator and knew the toxin was in that flask," he said. "If you count all the people in this building and in other labs all over campus who keep drugs in their refrigerators and could surmise you did, too, you're talking about hundreds of people."

"I could narrow that down by figuring out who would know how to administer a liquid toxin," said St. Clair.

Virginia shrugged. "Stir a drop into her iced tea."

"But how? It's not that easy to poison someone's drink. You have to know the person to get close enough. Nanette had to be eating with someone she knew, or she had to have drunk from something that someone poisoned ahead of time."

"You're talking about a husband," said Nathan. "Only a husband would know someone well enough to poison the right food."

"Or a friend," said St. Clair. "Doesn't she play tennis at

Spring Lawn? I've seen her out there. Everybody brings a thermos on hot days."

"Who does she play tennis with?" Nathan asked.

Virginia lifted a hand. "Guilty. I played with her a couple of times, but that's all. You knew her better than I did, Maxene."

"I only knew her through Hank. The parties I went to at her house were doctor parties."

Nathan opened another cracker package, spilling crumbs on the carpet. "Those parties are so dark and crowded, the toxin could have been dropped onto her hors d'oeuvres plate without anyone noticing."

Maxene shook her head. "If the poison were put into her drink or onto her food, the action would be almost immediate, even if she got only a few drops. Nanette would have died immediately. I'm amazed she got all the way to St. Agnes."

"She might have eaten it in a form that delayed digestion," suggested Nathan, "like in a capsule."

"True," said Virginia, "but that still means she was poisoned by someone who knew her well enough to give her something she would eat without hesitation. Or who could put it into a pill bottle in her medicine cabinet."

"Husband again," Nathan said.

St. Clair shook her head. "Hank had gone to Chicago that night."

"He could have put a capsule into a pill bottle anytime," Nathan said.

"Isn't that risky? What if she took it while he was there?"

"How did she get to St. Agnes?" Virginia cut in.

"Taxi."

Nathan picked up the thought. "That might be a lead. She got the cab because she was sick, right? So she had to have gotten sick somewhere near where the cab picked her up."

"I'll ask Detective Grabowski," St. Clair said. She jotted a note in her memo book for when she saw Grabowski again. If she saw him again. They hadn't parted on exactly friendly terms.

Virginia was gathering up her lecture notes for her next class.

"Tennis after you're off work tomorrow night, Max?" she asked as they walked down the hall. "Midnight courts are always open at the club. I'll be up until then, working on this stuff." She grimaced.

Maxene agreed, with mixed feelings. She used to play with Virginia once a week, but the game fell off when Maxene started suspecting Virginia of sleeping with Alan. At the time, she had suspected everyone.

Nathan trailed her to the building entrance. "Max," he said, "how much do you really know about Virginia's research?"

St. Clair stopped, surprised at the question. "She doesn't have much private life that I know of, she's so tied up in her research. She claims her research was what killed her marriage ten years ago, although I think she just told me that to make me feel better when I got divorced. She came out smelling like a rose from her divorce. She got the house, which is one of those cozy brick cottages that cost a quarter of a million. She can afford the mortgage from the grants she pulls in. She goes to a lot of faculty functions and doctor parties, but she always comes alone . . . claims she's too busy for relationships."

"Her research is coming up for review this year."

"That's just a formality with Virginia. Her research put this university on the map. Besides, I heard a rumor she's made a big breakthrough, although I may have heard that from Virginia."

Nathan lowered his voice. "I suspect that that rumor is just rumor. Virginia stopped doing any lab work a month ago. She told me she's through using the computer for statistical tabulation. But she still sits in her office going over her data, as if she's having trouble pulling it all together."

"She's writing another article. The woman has published more than anyone on campus."

"I think her grants have been cut, Maxene. You know that refrigerator and storage unit she wrote into her grant?

We should have had those six months ago."

"Payment is slow."

"Have you ever seen her data?"

"Of course not. No one has. She says if the newspapers ever found out about her research, the adverse publicity would make her life miserable." St. Clair pushed open the heavy doors. "Why are you so so suspicious, Nathan? Is this one of your anti-Virginia campaigns? You two have been at each other's throats for years. If you would just put on a clean shirt and shave, she would stop harassing you."

Nathan shrugged. "This has nothing to do with how she and I don't get along. She's been seeing Hank Myer. Lunches. Dinners. For months. Whenever she's out of her office, the switchboard operator rings her calls through to the lab, in case she's there. I picked it up a few times, and I recognized his voice."

"Dinners, lunches, so what?"

"Hank Myer is chairman of the Research Review Committee."

"So?"

"Maybe Virginia is trying to get in good with him."

"You're nuts. That's what graduate students do—not tenured faculty."

"Aren't you even curious, Max? What if she's in trouble? What if her grants have been cut? She's forty-five. That's too old to have her research completely fall apart, and have time to start over. I admit I'm getting my share of entertainment watching this little scenario, but I thought that since you have more innate sympathy in you than I do, you might want to help her out."

St. Clair hesitated. She had shared a lab with Virginia for years, and she liked her in a cautious way. And she was curious. Every researcher is curious about the methods of their successful colleagues. Everyone wants to know how much of their colleague's success was hard work and how much came from lucky flashes of intuition.

"First of all," she said, "forty-five is not old. But maybe she does need my help."

Back at St. Agnes, Dr. St. Clair detoured through the
lobby to use the pay phone. She propped her list of questions against the metal dome and read over her notes. First,
she would remind Grabowski how easy it was to pick the
locks on desk drawers. Second, she would ask where the
taxi had picked up Nanette. Third, she would find out if
Grabowski knew why Nanette was dressed like a hooker.
Finally, she would ask if he had located any other source
of tetrodotoxin in the city. With cheerful energy, she dialed
the Police Administration Building at Seventh and State.

The switchboard operator said Grabowski was out. St.
Clair left a message, feeling letdown. The operator had
taken her number, but Grabowski might not call. He had
been in a vile mood the night before. Why did he care that
she had supposedly slept with Hank Myer the night after his
wife's funeral? Male ego problem? Envy? Was the bereaved
husband a suspect? Or, of course, maybe her own actions
had moved her into first place in the line of suspects.

By 8:00 P.M., the flow of wounded had slowed enough for
her to grab dinner. She tossed her blood-smeared lab coat
into the hamper and detoured through Housekeeping for a
fresh one. The echoing, white-tiled hall smelled of laundry
soap, betadine, and the sharp tang of surgical anesthesia.
The cafeteria was up one floor: orange carpet, ochre walls,
fried hamburgers—a repellent place designed to send people scurrying out in half an hour. She ordered the special
without looking at it. Everything tasted the same. At a small
table in a quiet corner, she pulled out her list of questions
again. What could she add?

She was mulling it over when a heavy hand dropped on
her shoulder, and Hank Myer yanked out the opposite chair.
His lips were tight, and his jaw muscles bulged.

"Some Polack cop barged into my office today with a
crazy story about Nan not dying of a heart attack," he said,
his blue eyes like agates. "He said she was poisoned. He
also said you were the one who figured that out."

"Hank, I should have called you. I kept putting it off until
I knew something more definite."

"Whatever made you decide she was poisoned? She's buried. Can't we just leave her alone?"

"A healthy young woman with no history of heart disease suddenly drops dead of heart failure? It just isn't right."

"She had a systolic murmur."

"She was born with the heart murmur. Lots of people born with that live into their eighties."

"And lots don't. What the hell are you doing, Max?"

"Trying to establish a legitimate cause of death. Aaron Simonson had saved a blood sample from the autopsy and he suggested we send it to the AFIP for analysis."

"Aaron's idea?"

"Yes. Hank, why is this bothering you so much? Don't you want to find out what happened to her?"

"Why did you have to do this, Max? Nanette and I had our troubles, but I loved her, in my cold-hearted surgeon's way, as she always said. I loved her even though she said I made her feel like a victim. She said she was the victim of my surgery schedule, my on-call schedule. She said no matter what she did to get out of the victim mentality, I always did something to put her back in."

"A lot of women feel like they're victims of their husbands' careers."

"She said doctors are different. She said there's a reason why patients feel like victims when they have surgery, and that's because surgeons treat them like victims."

"And she died a victim of a poisoning."

He nodded. "I don't want people to remember her as a victim. She was trying to break out of that. Now she never will."

"I'm sorry, Hank."

He rubbed his face. "It's out of our hands now." He shoved back his chair, knocking against the table and tipping over Maxene's chocolate milk.

At midnight, St. Clair waved away the security guard and sprinted to her car, dodging unseen muggers. She felt terrible that Hank had to learn how his wife died from the police. She should have called him, she kept telling herself. She should have told him as soon as she knew. Her guilt feelings hardened her resolve to find out where the tetrodotoxin had come from. She wanted Hank to know it hadn't come from her.

She drove to her old lab building where Nathan was waiting. The building was as dark as it had been the night before. Her footsteps echoed through the hall and up the three long flights of stone steps to where the comforting ribbon of light from Nathan's lab stretched under the dark door.

Nathan raised a hand in conspiratorial silence, then reached into his filing drawer for flashlights. They crossed the dark hall to Virginia's office and listened. Even the creaks of the old building were silent. Nathan slid a credit card between the door and the lock, and they were quickly inside.

Maxene held the flashlight while Nathan began trying one key after another on the lock of the center desk drawer. The keys on the large ring jingled softly. At last he pulled open the drawer.

"I borrowed the janitor's keys while he was out," he muttered.

St. Clair settled herself on the floor, flashlight propped on her stomach, and opened the top folder that Nathan pulled out of the drawer. She didn't know exactly what to look for. The folder just held long columns of numbers, lab data like the sheets she had handed over to Grabowski. The columns represented test results from injecting mice with bacteria and the results of treating the infection with various strengths of agents. From the consistent low levels of response, it appeared that positive results were still some distance away.

She opened another notebook. It was a copy of Virginia's grant proposal, expense sheet attached. "I thought you said she didn't get a new refrigerator," St. Clair said.

"We didn't."

"What's this? Laboratory refrigerator, fifteen hundred dollars."

Nathan shone his flashlight on the page.

"Refrigerator, enclosed cabinets, one thousand laboratory mice," he read aloud. "It's been years since I smelled that many mice."

"Maybe she bought the refrigerator and cabinets for her home. It's been done before."

"The mice, too?" Nathan ran his fingers down the columns. "She's spending a lot of money. Test tubes, syringes, autoclave. Where is all this stuff? I haven't seen any of it."

St. Clair flashed her light on the page, but Nathan was stuffing the notebooks into the drawer. Footsteps were clicking down the hall. A key slid into the lock. Unbelieving, St. Clair froze. Nathan grabbed her arm and pulled her into the storage closet. They stood jammed together in darkness.

A stream of light shone under the closet door. Drawers opened and shut. A few minutes later, the lights switched off, the outer door closed, and footsteps sounded down the hall.

Maxene pushed open the closet door and drew a deep breath of less contaminated air. Her hands were shaking.

"What if that person had decided to open the closet door?" she whispered. "What if that person were the dean? It's midnight, and we're hiding inside a professor's closet, for God's sake."

Nathan was ignoring her. He scuttled over to the hall door and put his ear against the chipped wood. Then he hurried to the desk and, with both hands, quietly pulled open the drawer. It was empty.

Maxene stared into the shadowy depths, then, disbelieving, felt around inside. Nothing. Just the shadows and a faint, lingering scent of expensive perfume.

CHAPTER

8

MAXENE ST. CLAIR usually got up around 11:00. If she went to bed at 1:00 A.M., getting up after 10:00 made her feel she was working regular hours instead of hours nature never intended. For the first month, she felt dopey until mid-afternoon, but after a month her body got used to the night schedule.

Tonight she was playing tennis with Virginia at the club at midnight, and before then she was going to work a regular nine-hour shift at the ER. But never mind the stress and the sleep it required, it was a beautiful summer morning, birds were singing at 7:00 A.M., and St. Clair lay in bed wide awake. Crisp air drifted through the open window. The breeze off the lake rustled the elms. She got out of bed and peered up through the foliage. Cloudless skies. Too nice for sleep. It took only minutes to throw on a pair of shorts and pack some cola, sweet rolls, and her bathing suit into the front carrier of her bicycle. By 8:00 she was on her bicycle heading for the lake.

North Lake Drive rush-hour traffic was sluggish. She breezed through the line of cars at the stoplight and rode down the hill toward the waterfront park, where she picked up the bike path going south. A few other cyclers were out, several wearing the helmets and tight shorts of racers in training. Others were wearing office clothing and pedalling sedately toward work. The grass between the bike path and the lake was still trampled by the Fourth of July crowd. A few swimmers were wading into the lake. At McKinley Park beach, muscled young men were playing volleyball.

The water looked inviting, but she decided to bicycle further, to work up a sweat before plunging into the cold Lake Michigan water. Also, the South Shore Park beach was cleaner than this downtown one, and it was populated by mothers with children, an easier crowd to mingle with for a lone woman who didn't want to be constantly propositioned.

She cycled along the narrow streets under the East/West freeway where it ended at Lake Michigan, then crossed the narrow bridge onto South First Street, at the mouth of the waterway. On the other side of the bridge she passed through the blocks of hot, soot-encrusted factories of the south side waterfront. Tenements lined the right side of the street, warehouses the left. Between the warehouses, she caught glimpses of freighters tied up for loading. Shouts floated from the upper floor of a garment factory. The air hung heavy and thick, imprisoned between the warehouses and the ramshakle frame tenements. The lower windows of most of the tenements were boarded over. The buildings were still inhabited, though. As she cycled slowly by, skirting the trucks that were loading and unloading, she could see little faces peering through the chinks in the boards. Mexican immigrants followed the fruit harvest north and ended up in Milwaukee. They picked up a few crumbs of assembly-line work before heading their beat-up cars back across the Great Plains before winter hit. She had treated some of them at St. Agnes' ER, but usually they went to the free Catholic clinics and hospitals on the south side.

First Street became Kinnickinnic Avenue, which led her out of the factory district. At Russell Street, the bike route became a path again, winding through the miles of parks and beaches that ran along the lake. Across the street were bungalows with fat grinning porches topped by low peaked roofs. These Milwaukee bungalows filled the city, each with an unfenced patch of lawn in front and a garden with a clothesline in back. On the Polish south side, these bungalows were painted yellow, white, or bright blue. On the German north side, the bungalows were built of brick, asphalt shingles, or brown frame. In the densely populated north side Puerto Rican neighborhoods west of the river, where Joella lived, these same bungalows were painted pink, turquoise, or bright green.

St. Clair was bicycling slowly, taking in the unhurried sailboats and the swooping gulls, when she heard her name called. Across the untrafficked street, a man was lounging on the porch of a small white bungalow. His bare feet were propped on the porch rail. He saluted her with a beer can and stood up. It was Grabowski.

She stopped her bicycle and stared. Was this tanned man clad only in running shorts the same limply dressed cop who had been heaping abuse on her only the day before? She slowly pedalled across the street and dismounted on the weedy lawn.

"Want a beer?" Grabowski asked. He led the way into the house.

The front room was tidy but no one could accuse it of being furnished, Maxene thought. Previous tenants seemed to have abandoned their left-over furniture. A sagging green sofa, a recliner with a blanket over the seat, a TV with a VCR perched on it, and a small rag rug made up the ensemble. She followed Grabowski into a large kitchen with a round wooden table and two unmatched wooden chairs. The opposite door opened into a small bedroom with an unmade bed. Grabowski wrenched open the door of a refrigerator that looked like a converted icebox. He pulled out a Miller. The refrigerator held little else.

Maxene waved away the beer and poured herself a glass of water from the tap. On the counter lay a letter from Marquette University Law School. St. Clair moved the coffee cup that was sitting on it and read the short paragraph.

"What's this, Grabowski? Law school? It says here you're starting in the fall."

"That's what it says, all right."

"I'm confused. I thought you liked being a detective. I heard from the other police officers I sew up that you're a genius at it, rose in the ranks like a meteor."

"I don't know about meteors, but yes, I'm good at what I do. My lieutenant thinks I can be even better if I'm a detective and a lawyer at the same time."

"What do you think?"

"Depends on the day."

St. Clair leaned against the counter and took a sip of water. It tasted like yeast—a hazard of living in a brewery town. "You already know how the criminal mind works. Are you trying to find out how the criminal lawyer mind works? You want to be as devious as they are?"

He shrugged. "You think it's a good idea? It's the great American dream: get another degree and rush out to buy three-piece suits."

"Aside from the hideous thought of you in a three-piece suit, I'm not sure if becoming a lawyer is moving up in the world. You're smart enough to be a lawyer, of course. Smarter, if my experience facing lawyers on the expert witness stand is any basis for judgment. The problem is, you might change, even if you stayed a detective. You'd get argumentative."

"Would not."

"Would too."

He grinned. "Maybe I would be a laid-back lawyer who wore wrinkled seersucker."

"Maybe."

Back on the porch, he propped his feet on the rail.

"Let's go away for the weekend when this is all over," he said abruptly. "Let's go to Gilroy and take the Wisconsin bike trail. There's a nice little hotel about thirty miles down the track."

St. Clair took a sip of water. "Does this mean I'm no longer a suspect, despite my irregular behavior?"

"You never were a suspect for me, Maxene, although I wish you could prove it. So far, all you've done is incriminate yourself."

"Let me make up for it. Maybe I can find things out for you."

He rolled his eyes. "No amateur detecting, please. You'll get hurt."

"The murder happened in my world, Grabowski. Nanette Myer was a doctor's wife, the poison came from a medical research lab, and a doctor—me—figured out what poison it was. Your only suspect is a doctor—also me. I knew Nanette socially, and I know all the doctors involved. I'm a perfect person to tie seemingly unrelated facts together for you."

"We're dealing with a murderer, Maxene. This isn't your field, and it could be dangerous."

"Those two phrases have kept women out of men's professions for too long. My great-aunt was told those phrases her entire life, but fortunately she ignored them. To get into medical school, she had to pledge she would not marry, then she had to live in the nurse's dormitory under the supervision of a head nurse who made her wear starched white collars and cuffs. After she graduated, she once again ignored those phrases and went to India to work for missionary hospitals. I never heard her complain that her profession wasn't a woman's field or that it was too dangerous."

"I wasn't trying to be sexist."

"It is sexist, and so is medicine," St. Clair said. "Medicine is a big men's club, no matter how many women enter it. Women doctors learn to accept the isolated feeling of playing on someone else's turf, so we tend to do things for ourselves, instead of going to male doctors for approval or support. To ask a male medical student for help was to risk being treated like a helpless female. If I could survive medicine, I can survive this investigation."

Grabowski rolled the beer across his forehead. The act had to come from frustration, Maxene realized, because it wasn't hot enough on the breezy porch to warrant that typical Milwaukee hot-weather gesture.

"I need help from somewhere," Grabowski admitted. "This is the tightest-lipped group I've ever had the misfortune to interrogate. I've interviewed half a dozen of Nanette Myer's friends—all doctors' wives—along with a handful of doctors. All I get are polite evasions. They all knew the victim, they know she died wearing the clothes of a prostitute, they know she came to an inner-city emergency room where she had no business being, yet none of them will even speculate out loud."

St. Clair laughed. "Let me guess. The doctors' wives invited you into their interior-decorated, air-conditioned homes, served you iced tea with mint leaves, smiled sweetly with their hands folded in their laps, and told you exactly nothing."

Grabowski squinted at her. "Why aren't you like them? You live in what they would call a dump, you don't wear designer dresses, although if you did, you'd look like a million bucks, and you work like a dog."

"I'd love to own one of those gorgeous homes, but research medicine doctors don't make that kind of money. No, I take that back. Virginia makes a bundle, but she works longer hours than Hank Myer."

Grabowski sighed. "I have too much other work to waste time waiting for rich folks to drop morsels from their lips."

St. Clair grinned. "Answer my questions, and I'll tell you all my conclusions. First, where did the taxi pick up Nanette to bring her to St. Agnes'?"

"On Twenty-first Street south of North Avenue, toward Elm Elementary School."

"What was she doing?"

"No idea. She was dressed like a hooker, but the taxi driver said she was alone when she flagged him down."

"Did anyone in the neighborhood see her?"

"If they did, they're not telling. It's a black neighborhood, and that particular area is mostly prostitutes and pimps. Nobody talks to cops without coercion."

"Don't you have plainclothesmen there?"

"Sure, but they're on drug detail. We spend less time busting prostitutes than the good people of Milwaukee think. Every once in a while we round up a bunch to keep the mayor happy. No one on drug detail heard anything about Nanette, which means she wasn't pushing or dealing."

"That's a relief."

They sat in silence. Finally Grabowski touched her arm. "I get the feeling you know something about this case you're not telling."

"I feel odd telling you. Disloyal to my profession."

He groaned. "What is it about doctors that makes them act like there's a conspiracy against them? Do me a favor. Pretend you're not a member of a big medical club that never testifies against one another in court."

St. Clair flushed. "There is good reason why doctors close ranks when one of us gets accused of malpractice. A lot of medicine is pure guesswork. We try a treatment; if it doesn't work, we try something else. But patients and their families want to believe that doctors know everything. When something goes wrong—and it often does—patients want the doctor to be responsible. They can't tolerate the idea that medicine is an art, not a science. So doctors keep their mouths shut when things go wrong with another doctor's patient. It was probably an accident of nature and had nothing to do with poor medical care."

"Have you ever kept mum when you knew a doctor screwed up?"

"Yes. But among ourselves, doctors know what's a screwup and what's an unavoidable accident of nature."

"And when it's a screwup, you turn in the offender to the state medical society?"

"Well, not often," St. Clair admitted.

Grabowski sighed. "Tell me what you've heard via this secret medical grapevine. I'm not going to expose your sources by broadcasting your hunches."

St. Clair hesitated. "What I heard sounds like I'm starting malicious gossip, and there's already enough of that in the medical community."

"Let me decide."

"Hank Myer stopped by the hospital last night. He was upset that you had opened this investigation."

"Why?"

"He said it was unnecessary, that she had a congenital murmur that caused her death. He didn't want anything done further. I can understand how he feels; it's a normal reaction."

"Unless he knows something more about why she died."

St. Clair didn't answer.

"Tell me about Virginia Gaust." He changed the subject. "You shared a lab with her, didn't you? What does she do at the university?"

"She has an M.D. degree plus a Ph.D. in pharmacology. She spends most of her time on her research but she's also head of the department of pharmacology. That position is passed around among tenured faculty. It's more work than status, although Virginia seems to enjoy the faculty entertaining that goes with it. Dinner with the dean, and all that."

"She does research and also organizes the department?"

"And teaches a course for medical students. The Medical College of Wisconsin science faculty is pulled from the Marquette science departments. We all taught one class per semester for them, as well as taught at Marquette, and kept up our research. Virginia likes teaching. She's brilliant, and everything comes easily."

"You sound envious."

St. Clair thought that over. "Virginia works harder and longer hours than anybody I know. She's obsessed with her research. She's at the lab nights, weekends, holidays. I envy her singlemindedness, but more, I envy her flashes of intuition. I rarely get those leaps of understanding; few researchers do."

"What's her research?"

St. Clair hesitated long enough that Grabowski touched her arm. She jumped. "Can you keep this quiet? It's no secret, but Virginia likes to maintain a low profile."

"To keep her ideas from being stolen?"

"More for the campus peace of mind. She's researching drugs to cure leprosy."

"Leprosy!" Grabowski recoiled. St. Clair laughed.

"Don't be so biblical. Leprosy is treatable. It's just another chronic bacterial disease."

"Then why is Dr. Gaust looking for a new drug?"

"I shouldn't have spoken so quickly. Leprosy is treatable in this country. But in the last few years, the drought in Africa and India, combined with the border wars they keep having, have reduced the population's resistance to disease. Diseases that everyone thought were stamped out, or at least under control, are showing up again. Smallpox and bubonic plague both spread in Southeast Asia during the Vietnam years, and they're spreading again in Africa. Leprosy is also increasing."

"Why do they need a new drug if leprosy is treatable?"

"Over time, leprosy bacteria become resistant to current drugs. Lots of bacteria resist treatment after a while. Leprosy was originally treated with a bacteriostatic drug called Dapsion, which stopped the bacterial advance but didn't kill it. It didn't take long for strains of leprosy to become resistant. The same happened to Clofazinine, which is weakly bacteriocidal and was never that effective, even without resistance problems. Rifampin was the drug of choice after that. Now the World Health Organization recommends treating leprosy with all three."

"So what's the problem? Why can't they stamp out this recent rise in leprosy?"

"Cases are being reported that resist all three drugs, even in combination. Normally, about eleven million leprosy cases are reported yearly. Now the numbers are three times that and increasing. That means current cases aren't responding to therapy, plus additional cases are being discovered."

"Are you talking epidemic?"

"Not like when my great-aunt was working in Indian hospitals. But Dr. Singh, an Indian doctor who works at the North Avenue Public Health Clinic, tells me the Indian government has reopened some old leper colonies. My aunt used to work in one of them. She was so happy when it closed; now it's open again. It's temporary, but it's a step backward."

"What's the situation in this country? Surely it's no problem here."

"I haven't kept up with it since I stopped working in the same lab with Virginia every day, but Dr. Singh said she spotted a case in the inner-city clinic earlier this summer. A woman from Chicago brought her baby to clinic and Dr. Singh spotted leprosy sores on the woman. A public-health nurse immediately drove the mother and baby downtown to the infectious disease clinic for treatment. The family were immigrants from India. They were the only case, as far as I know, but I haven't talked to Dr. Singh recently."

"Is Dr. Gaust close to finding a new drug?"

"I heard she is." St. Clair started to add what Nathan had said about Virginia's research, then decided not to. Nathan's opinion of Virginia wasn't reliable. "Even if she has a new drug, it has to be approved by the FDA and other federal agencies, which can take years. With a leprosy drug, it could take decades. Leprosy bacteria won't live in a test tube, so Virginia can't just smear some bacteria on a slide and pour her solution over it to see if the bacteria die. Leprosy bacteria only survive inside a human. Since using humans for experiments is nearly impossible in this country, Virginia has had to go through years of testing on mice footpads, then hope the FDA will accept empirical data."

"Mice footpads?" Grabowski grimaced.

"She grows the leprosy bacteria on the footpads of mice, then kills the mice, grinds up the footpads, and treats it with her new drug. The method doesn't work well."

"You said she draws more research money than anyone at the university. What does that mean?"

"Each university gets research money from government and private sources, like philanthropies or drug companies. The Research Review Committee decides which researcher gets it. Most of the time, though, drug companies or other private sources give the money to a certain researcher, who then has to give a big percentage back to the university for

administrative costs. The more money a researcher attracts
to the university, the more money goes to the university,
which they use to fund other departments. The university
rewards the researcher with titles, a nice lab, paid confer-
ences abroad, other perks. It's a pleasant life, as long as the
research is going well. When the research sours, the money
and perks dry up."

"But researchers whose work isn't going well need the
money as much as those whose work is going well."

"More. Sometimes the Research Review Committee will
have enough faith in a researcher to keep funds coming until
results improve." Maxene finished her water in silence, then
she remembered she didn't know why Grabowski had asked
about Virginia.

"Oh," he said, peering into his beer suds, "Myer's car
was seen outside her home on several occasions since his
wife died. All night."

"Pleading loneliness," she said bitterly. "Saying he only
had her to turn to in his hour of grief."

Grabowski looked carefully at the horizon. "Dirty double-
dealing two-timer."

St. Clair smiled despite herself. "He's old enough to
spend his nights wherever he wants."

"He's on Dr. Gaust's Research Review Committee,
Nathan mentioned," Grabowski commented. "Aren't their
little trysts a conflict of interest?"

"Who cares?" St. Clair said, and went inside to change
into her swimming suit. She spent the next half hour gasping at the frigid lake water, not caring about anything except
sand and sun.

She bicycled home a short while after, marveling at how
Grabowski managed to emerge clean from the mess that
was his bathroom. By the time she got home, changed, ate,
and raced to St. Agnes, the patients were piling up. First on
the list was Lavelle Taylor, the highest-earning prostitute of
the highest-earning pimp, Rolondo.

CHAPTER

9

ROLONDO APPEARED EVERY few weeks at St. Agnes ER with one of his ladies who had met misadventure at someone's hands, probably his own, St. Clair had long since decided.

"What happened?" she asked, as always, staring with sympathy and horror at the carmel-colored beat-up face of Lavelle Taylor, who was lying on the exam table, hands folded over her flat stomach. Lavelle's hair was plaited into neat corn rows, but the rest of her face was not so tidy. Blood had smeared her purple eye shadow and discolored the scarlet lipstick. Being a well-trained prostitute, Lavelle kept her lips sealed so her pimp could do the talking. Except that he wasn't talking. He was lounging on the neighboring exam table swinging his legs, occasionally stretching out one foot to admire the crease in his white linen slacks and the shine on his white leather pumps.

St. Clair gestured to Shirley to open a suture kit onto the metal tray table. She held up her hands for the sterile gloves, then picked out a cotton ball soaked in Betadine and started scrubbing Lavelle's chin and lower lip. She glanced over at Rolondo, who was staring at the ceiling.

"You going to tell me how this happened?" She took the syringe of lidocaine from Shirley and slowly inserted the needle into Lavelle's lip.

"No."

She dropped the syringe on the tray and leaned against the table waiting for the anesthesia to do its work. Shirley handed her some forceps with a curved needle and suture clamped in them. After a minute, St. Clair took a careful first stitch.

St. Clair's suturing skills had improved over the last six months. She had spent ten hours watching a plastic surgeon at work, to remind herself of the tricks of attaching separate layers of skin in the right order. Then she had taken up surgeons' hobbies of knitting, crocheting, and tying surgical knots in the dark. The homework was paying off. The tear in Lavelle's lip was closing nicely. She tied off the last stitch and dropped the needle into the suture kit.

Rolondo jumped off the exam table and leaned over Lavelle to peer at the finished job. "Good work, Doc. Here. Take yourself out to dinner." He dropped a fifty-dollar bill onto the metal tray table.

"I'm already well paid, thanks," St. Clair said, peeling off her gloves and tossing them into the used suture set.

"I know how you paid, and it ain't well. My ladies make more in one night than you make in a week."

St. Clair resisted the urge to ask how much his ladies kept for themselves. She glanced down at Lavelle, who smiled crookedly around the sutures. Maxene picked up the fifty and clipped it to the chart. "St. Anthony's poor box will appreciate the donation."

Rolondo had seated himself again at the end of the exam table, studying a scuff mark on one white shoe. St. Clair began feeling over Lavelle's arms and legs for possible fractures, something she always did for prostitutes, no matter why they came into the ER.

"Say," Rolondo said. "What happened to Mae West? I seen her leave here dead about a week ago. I was in here with one of my ladies, but you didn't see me. You was busy with Mae West."

"Mae West?" St. Clair had found a rash between Lavelle's fingers that looked like scabies. "Does this itch?" she asked.

"That ain't her real name, I know," Rolondo continued, "but that's what she went by. Kinky lady."

"I can't remember anyone by that name." St. Clair turned Lavelle's hands over and glanced up her arms. A collection of needle marks had discolored the inside of the elbow. St. Clair scowled.

Rolondo was continuing. "You had the whole crowd in here with you, zapping her with wires, shooting her up. I never seen so many needles, even on the street."

St. Clair stopped looking at the needle marks and concentrated on what Rolondo was saying. "Are you talking about a white woman? Short black hair. Red wig?"

"That's her. You had the curtains open so you all could get around her. I seen her face real clear. And every other part of her, too. You folks should watch out for people's privacy. My lady almost fainted when she seen what you was doing to that poor woman."

"You sure this happened last week? We only had one white woman die here last week and her name wasn't Mae West."

"I know who I'm talking about and when I seen her." An annoyed frown creased Rolondo's broad brow. "I seen her when you was beating on her, and I seen her when you pulled that sheet over her. It was Mae West. What'd she die of? Not AIDS, was it?"

St. Clair struggled to understand. Was he talking about Nanette Myer? "How do you know her name was Mae West?"

"First you tell me what she died of. Then I tell you all about her."

"It's a long story." She was about to launch into it when Shirley stuck her head through the curtains and held up her hand.

"They're stacking up out here, Doctor," she snapped. "You about finished?"

St. Clair helped Lavelle sit up. "I have to talk to you about this Mae West," she said to Rolondo. "Can we meet somewhere?"

"Luigi's Italian Deli," he said, unexpectedly. "You know where it's at. I seen you eating in there before."

"Across from the North Avenue Public Health Clinic?"

"Any day around noon. One of my ladies will find me."

He pushed aside the curtains, holding them a fraction of a second for Lavelle, then sauntered toward the door. He flipped a few bills onto the receptionist's desk. Lavelle trudged behind him, unsteady on her recklessly high heels, shaky from the anesthesia. The electric doors opened, and they vanished into the night.

"Mae West?" hissed Shirley. "That pimp couldn't mean Mrs. Myer, could he? She was the only white woman who died here last week."

"Forget you heard him. Tomorrow I'll find out who he was talking about. Maybe I can find some photo of Nanette Myer and see if he recognizes her."

"You think Mrs. Myer was hooking? Holy Jesus! I wonder what other diseases she carried."

Shirley pulled the curtains around another exam table, and for the next two hours, St. Clair forgot all about Nanette Myer.

At 11:45 the ER was empty again. Al Malech, the doctor who covered the midnight to 8:00 A.M. shift, arrived early, so St. Clair threw her stained white coat into a laundry hamper, grabbed her tennis bag out of the locker in the women's lounge, and sprinted to the parking lot. The sprint got her blood moving and opened her drooping eyes. At this rate she would be wider awake than Virginia, and she might win the match, unless Virginia had sneaked in an afternoon nap.

The Spring Lawn Tennis Club was dark except for one light over the vacant receptionist's desk. Virginia's car wasn't there yet, a surprise. Despite a seemingly casual attitude toward schedules and deadlines, Virginia had never been late for anything. St. Clair pushed open the front door and walked down the empty corridor into the even more empty women's dressing room.

The cold flicker of the fluorescent light made the room cold and uninviting. She sat tentatively on a bench, uneasy at the thought of disrobing in the eerie silence. If Virginia didn't show up in ten minutes, she would go home to bed.

Five minutes ticked by. Finally, she heard the locker-room door click open.

"Virginia?" she called. A bank of lockers blocked her view of the door, and she heard no footsteps rounding the corner, no clang of a locker opening.

"Virginia?" She cleared her throat, annoyed at the tremor. She walked cautiously around the bank of lockers, then stopped in surprise. Facing her was a ball machine, the kind that mechanically shoots tennis balls at players who want to practice a certain stroke. The machine hummed quietly, plugged into a wall socket.

"How did that get in here?" she exclaimed aloud, stepping toward it.

It was an unfortunate move. As she stepped into range, a green tennis ball dropped neatly into the maw of the machine. In a split second it fired.

Out of the mouth of the catapult, a bare two feet away, the ball shot into the air and smashed into St. Clair's mouth. She cried out and staggered backward, tripping over a bench in front of a line of lockers. Another ball dropped into the mouth and shot toward her. It smashed into the side of her head. She fell backward over the bench, hitting her head against a locker. She crawled to her feet, trying to get out of range.

Another ball rolled relentlessly into the mouth of the machine. Click. Pain blasted her forehead. Another ball missed her, crashed instead into the locker. She tried to crawl away but the balls seemed to follow. They were coming faster, although that wasn't possible, her brain tried to tell her. Balls came at the speed set on the machine, unless someone raised the speed. No one had come in. Or had they?

"Ooof!" Another ball hit her on the side of the neck, propelling her into the lockers, wrenching her shoulders. She collapsed in a heap on the floor, trying to wriggle under the bench. Then something hit her on the back of the head, and everything went dark.

When she woke up, there was a humming noice inside her head, and voices were coming from above her.

"It looks like she's coming around," said someone who sounded like Grabowski, even over the humming noise.

St. Clair moaned.

"How could she get hit by a ball machine at this time of the night!" Virginia's voice sounded perplexed and anxious. "In the locker room? What was that awful machine doing in here?"

St. Clair tried to open her eyes, but could only manage one. Someone had turned on all the lights. They blasted into her like midday sun. The humming inside her head was louder. It drowned out the voices. She couldn't make out what people were saying. Someone laid a wet washcloth over her eyes and slid something under head. Grabowski.

"Take it easy," he said. His voice was louder than the others, or maybe the humming was fading. "Hold this cloth over your face until the Aid Unit gets here."

St. Clair peered around the washcloth. Her face was one throbbing pain. Her head felt like someone had broken a tennis racket over it. "Grabowski," she muttered. He wasn't listening.

"Who turned on that ball machine?" he was demanding. His voice was harsh.

A babble of voices began interrupting each other. The receptionist began explaining how she had only left for a few minutes. A sweaty woman tennis player laid her white sweater over Maxene. Then the locker-room door banged and two medics pushed everyone aside and started feeling her body. They got to her neck and stopped.

"Can you talk?" one asked.

"Yes." The word found its way past bleeding and swollen lips.

"Can you see my fingers? How many am I holding up?"

St. Clair concentrated on the wavering, blurred fingers. "Two. No, three. My face hurts." She tried to sit up.

The medics peered into her eyes, wiped some blood off her face.

"She's probably all right," one said to Grabowski, "but you should take her to an emergency room. St. Agnes is closest, if you don't mind an inner-city hospital."

"Home," St. Clair said.

"Suit yourself." The medic shrugged. "There's nothing wrong with St. Agnes. Lots of white people go there. The doctors are no worse than anywhere else."

The janitor was babbling excuses. "I just went into the other building to repair a net. When I came out, someone had moved the ball machine out of the storeroom. I didn't even know where it went until I heard the lady screaming."

St. Clair couldn't remember screaming, but she decided not to mention her memory loss. "I'm not suing," she promised. "Take me home."

Grabowski put her into his car, after a whispered conference with Virginia who wanted to take her to her house. They compromised. Grabowski would take her to her own apartment, and Virginia would come along to make sure she was all right.

St. Clair leaned her head against the cool plastic headrest and closed her eyes. She was slipping into sleep when she felt herself being picked up. The sensation wasn't unpleasant. Nice to have someone get her up the stairs without her having to walk. Grabowski negotiated the hallway to the bedroom and lowered her onto cool sheets.

In a few minutes, Virginia woke her out of a doze. She felt Virginia's fingers folding her fist around a glass. "Tylenol with codeine from your medicine cabinet," Virginia said, forcing a large pill into her mouth.

St. Clair choked it down, thinking how easy it would be to poison a person who trusted you. As she drifted back to sleep, she could feel Virginia gently placing an ice pack on her swollen and throbbing face.

CHAPTER

10

BREEZE-TOSSED LEAVES WERE kaleidoscoping patterns on the window shade when St. Clair awoke. She could smell the faint fishy aroma of Lake Michigan in midsummer. She peered at the clock through the only eye that would open. Nearly noon. The humming was gone from inside her head, and she could hear sparrows chirping in her neighbor's birdbath. She tried to sit up to look at herself in the bureau mirror, but stopped when every muscle screamed out with pain.

She watched the dappled shadows dance on the shade and thought over what had happened. Who could have turned on the ball machine so it spat out tennis balls at the precise moment she was standing in front of it? Was it an accident or did someone watch her go into the locker room, then deliberately push the machine inside and turn on the switch? The lag when the machine dropped the first ball into the trigger slot would give a curious person in the locker room just enough time to walk within firing range. Who besides a tennis player would know that? She wondered if Virginia or Grabowski had seen anyone leaving the club. What was Grabowski doing there? All this was too much. St. Clair groaned.

The bedroom door opened, and Grabowski poked in his head. "Breakfast?" he asked, too cheerfully, St. Clair thought. "First, I'll get you another ice pack."

She heard the freezer door bang, then he reappeared, wrapping a blue cold pack in a dish towel. He picked the thawed cold pack off her pillow.

"Have you been here all night?" St. Clair was suddenly aware she was wearing her nightshirt.

"I slept on the couch."

St. Clair covered her face with the dish towel.

At 2:00 P.M., Shirley, head nurse in the ER that night, called. Grabowski took the call in the kitchen, then yelled at Maxene to pick it up in the bedroom. He watched her while she talked. Shirley's voice sounded reassuringly familiar.

"I found a surgery resident to cover the ER," Shirley said. "He can't do too much damage."

"I forgot all about work," St. Clair muttered, half-asleep.

"Did a doctor check you over?" Shirley sounded worried. "That good-looking Polack said you looked awful—blood all over your face and eyes swollen shut. It's a wonder you didn't lose a tooth, or an eye, God forbid. What kind of place is that tennis club?"

"Stop worrying. I'll be back at work tomorrow." St. Clair hitched herself up in bed and caught sight of her purple and swollen features in the mirror. "I think." She handed the phone to Grabowski and closed her eyes.

At 6:00 she woke again and pulled herself out of bed. Grabowski was sitting at her kitchen table reading a pile of reports. St. Clair leaned against the doorjamb, waiting for her knees to steady. Grabowski looked up. His gray eyes widened.

"Should you be up?"

"I'm tired of bed."

St. Clair wrapped her robe around her more securely and peered into the mirror that hung over the sink. One eye was magenta and had swollen to twice its size. The other was normal size, but blood had drained into the area below her eye, turning it purple. A subconjunctival hemorrhage in the left eye had turned the sclera red. Her nose and cheeks were lumpy with raised round welts, and her upper lip was split vertically. She tottered to a kitchen chair.

"What happened? Who turned on that ball machine?" she demanded.

"No one seems to know. It's the weirdest accident I've ever seen." He reached behind him into the refrigerator for a can of Miller and cracked it open. He handed it to her. "From what we can reconstruct, someone pushed the ball machine into the women's locker room after you went in there, then turned it on. Whether it was intended to hit you, I can't guess. Whoever did it must have left by a back door, because the receptionist didn't see anyone leaving between the time you went in and the time Virginia went into the locker room. Of course, the receptionist wasn't at the desk the whole time. She came back from the bathroom a few minutes after Virginia arrived. I was just behind her."

St. Clair held the cold beer against her eye. She felt dizzy. "You think somebody aimed that machine at me deliberately? Why?" She put her head down on the table.

Grabowski patted her arm. "I don't know whether it was deliberate or if you were the intended victim. Go back to bed."

"Say," she said. "What were you doing there, anyway? Are you following me around like I'm a suspect?"

"I got a message that you called when I was in my car, so I decided to drive over and talk to you in person. Your replacement told me you were playing tennis. Aren't you glad I came by?"

"Am I or am I not a suspect?"

"My lieutenant thinks the evidence points your way, Max: means, method, and apparently, motive."

"But someone tried to kill me."

"With a ball machine? Skeptics among the police are claiming you turned it on yourself."

"They're crazy. Do you know why I don't think this was an accident? Because I feel like a victim. People don't feel like victims unless they're treated like victims." She took a tentative sip of beer, stinging her cracked lips. She poured it into a glass and carefully drank half of it. She staggered back to bed.

Alcohol and narcotics taken in combination will put a person out permanently, unless it's only half a beer and one Tylenol with codeine. St. Clair woke up six hours later feeling hungry. It was midnight. A tour revealed Grabowski stretched out on the living room floor in a sleeping bag, several empty beer cans within arms' reach. She wondered if Grabowski's bedroom was knee-deep in cans. She wandered around the apartment, stretching her stiff muscles, then ate a carton of yogurt and went back to bed.

At noon the next day, she woke up feeling ready to spend time somewhere else besides bed. No police were sleeping in her living room or snacking in her kitchen. Grabowski must have decided a nursemaid was no longer needed. Which is fine, she thought, carefully testing each arm and finding them stiff but free of pain. She rinsed off in a cool shower. She had told Shirley she would be at work at 3:00 P.M., which left time to meet Rolondo at Luigi's cafe. There was no need to tell Grabowski where she was going. A police detective could be a real inhibitor in a meeting with a pimp. And besides, Grabowski's watchdog attitude was insulting her independence.

A cup of coffee and four aspirin raised her energy level further. She rummaged through a box of snapshots and found several of Nanette Myer at one of her pool parties. St. Clair stuffed the photos into her purse, carefully put on the largest pair of dark glasses she owned, and walked slowly out to her car. Grabowski had brought it home for her. Probably driven by the efficient Sergeant Lemie.

Luigi's Italian Deli was the best Italian restaurant in Milwaukee, for those with courage enough to find it among the boarded up storefronts between Twenty-first and Twenty-second streets on North Avenue. Diners also had to find a parking place in an area jammed with winos, prostitutes, and gangs of truant black adolescents. Luigi's was always crowded. Cadillacs double-parked in front, motors running, while elegantly dressed men lounged among the women strolling along the hot, gritty sidewalk.

St. Clair parked in the shade around the corner on Twenty-first Street and walked slowly toward Luigi's. She spotted Lavelle slouched in a doorway down the block. Lavelle waved a casual hand, then said something to a child who was breaking into a nearby parked car. The child sprinted athletically through traffic and burst into an open doorway near a broken storefront window. At the upper window, a blue gingham curtain twitched.

"How are you, Lavelle?" St. Clair lifted her dark glasses so she could better see the stitches in Lavelle's swollen lip.

"Just fine, honey." Lavelle peered at St. Clair's black and blue face. "You shouldn't let no man do that to you."

"I couldn't agree more."

A patrol car drifted by, slowing as it passed. Lavelle gave the officers a friendly nod. St. Clair moved away, not wanting to ruin Lavelle's trade, or get caught up in it. She ducked through the ropes of garlic draping the doorway of Luigi's and slid into a window booth.

Rolondo appeared before her iced tea did. He was wearing a purple satin shirt and cream gabardine pants. He carried the matching jacket over his shoulder, a fashion concession to the heat wave. His calfskin shoes had higher heels than St. Clair's. He slid into the booth without a greeting and pulled open the blue curtains. He was watching three black girls sharing shade on the cement steps of an apartment building across the street. On this blistering day they wore skin-tight red leather minis and leather boots. When they saw Rolondo watching them, they dragged themselves off the porch and started strolling down the street. The squad car drifted by again, veering slightly to miss three children jumping rope in an empty parking spot. The jumper in the middle turned to watch the patrol car pass without missing a step.

Luigi poured two glasses of iced tea, wiped his hands on his once white apron, and pulled an order pad out of his pocket. Not a hint of surprise had crossed his fleshy face at the sight of a St. Agnes doctor lunching with the neighborhood's most affluent pimp. St. Clair mentally added him to her lengthening list of people to cross-examine.

"The usual," Rolondo said, letting the curtain drop.

St. Clair peered at the menu from behind her dark glasses. "Basket of fried zucchini."

"Watch that fried stuff," warned Rolondo, glancing at her waistline. "You be off the market before you even on."

"I am not on any market," St. Clair said stiffly. "I enjoy being divorced."

"If you ain't available, how come you got all those marks on your face?"

"I was attacked," St. Clair snapped. "Someone tried to kill me with a tennis-ball machine. That's a machine that shoots balls at you in case you don't have a partner."

"I know what it is. I play tennis every Wednesday at my club." An irritated crease appeared in Rolondo's brow. "That why that cop's following you?"

St. Clair smacked open the curtain and glared up and down the busy street. Another patrol car cruised by, but no unmarked patrol car with Grabowski at the wheel. "No one is following me," she said.

Rolondo leaned back in the booth. A gold tooth gleamed in the blue filtered light. "Ain't nobody out there. I was just checking if you were working with the cops."

"The thought is claustrophobic."

"Okay, Okay." He lit a slender brown cigarette. "Talk to me about Mae West. How'd she die?"

"Poison. Nothing contagious."

"Who poisoned her?"

"I don't know, and that's my problem. The poison that killed her probably came from my research lab at Marquette, and she died in my ER, under my hands, so to speak."

Rolondo's gold tooth gleamed. "The cops think you killed her? You couldn't kill a louse if it was crawling on you."

"What a delightful image. But you see my position. If I can find who poisoned her, I can put an end to this whole question. So, would you look at this photo and tell me if this is the same woman you called Mae West?"

Rolondo glanced at it without touching it. He yawned. "That's the lady. Mae West."

"How do you know? The very idea is preposterous!"

"I seen her. On the street."

"What do you mean, 'on the street'?"

Rolondo half smiled. "How well you know the lady?"

"She's the wife of a doctor I work with. I've been to parties at her house. Look, here are more pictures. Her at her house, for God's sake."

Rolondo's gaze passed over the photos, casual disinterest. He picked one up to look at it more closely, then dropped it again: "So she's the fancy wife of a fancy doctor. And you don't know what 'on the street' means?"

"Are you saying she was a prostitute?"

"She was working the street. Make up your own mind."

"But that's absurd, Rolondo. If she wanted illicit sex, she had the whole medical community!"

Rolondo shrugged. "I don't know about action in the medical community, as you call it, but I do know about action on the street. And that's where this lady was. On the street." He smiled.

St. Clair felt her face flush. "Why do I get the feeling you're having a private joke? Tell me straight. Was she or was she not a prostitute?"

"Take it easy, doc. She wasn't no prostitute. All she did was give me a couple hundred bucks to let her hang around with Lavelle a few times. I was to keep her from being hassled."

"Why did she want to hang around with Lavelle?"

"She said she was writing a book. A honky excuse for a cheap thrill, is how I see it. But it was her money."

St. Clair set her teeth. "If you were keeping an eye on her, how did she get poisoned?"

Rolondo's gaze moved sideways, and his smirk faded. A tall figure blocked the end of the booth. Detective Grabowski had tracked St. Clair down.

CHAPTER

11

GRABOWSKI SLID INTO the booth next to Maxene and reached for a piece of fried zucchini. "Since you forgot to tell me where you were going, I called Shirley at St. Agnes. She said this little meeting might have something to do with Nanette Myer."

"I don't have nothing to hide," Rolondo said.

"That'll be the day."

"Look." Rolondo leaned forward. "I want to help out this nice lady doctor. She patches up my girls, and she don't ask too many questions. Now she tells me you're on her case about this Mae West business. I don't like that. I need Dr. Maxene to keep being the night doctor at St. Agnes'. I'll tell you what you want, but she didn't have nothing to do with that woman dying, and neither did I."

"I haven't arrested Dr. St. Clair or you for anything. Yet," Grabowski said. "Now fill me in."

Grabowski didn't raise an eyebrow during Rolondo's brief review. "How often did she wander along North Avenue pretending to be a prostitute?" he asked finally.

"Three or four times over a couple of months."

"Was she into drugs?"

Rolondo shook his head, preoccupied with his chilled Fettuccini Alfredo.

"You sure?"

"Sure he's sure," St. Clair hastily intervened. A slight frown had appeared on the pimp's calm face. "He keeps close watch on his, er, ladies. How else could he stay in business?"

Grabowski looked at her a few seconds longer than necessary. He turned back to Rolondo. "Did she ever let herself get picked up?"

"Once or twice. She left with a white dude."

"What did he look like?"

"I never seen the guy. Mae West stuck with Lavelle and the other girls."

"I thought she paid you to watch out for her."

Rolondo shrugged.

Grabowski scowled. "I have trouble believing that a wealthy doctor's wife would go into prostitution at the rates they pay on this street."

"Rates ain't bad," Rolondo said, signaling for more iced tea.

St. Clair cut in. "She never did anything anyway."

Grabowski sighed. "Lavelle says she left with a white man."

"But that was someone she knew."

"What makes you say that?"

"She wouldn't leave with someone she didn't know, would she?"

Grabowski frowned at her. "A woman who would come to North Avenue dressed like a prostitute might just take it into her head to act like one, don't you think?"

St. Clair fought down indignation and tried to consider the situation objectively. Would a wealthy doctor's wife actually have sex for money with a stranger she picked up in the worst part of town? She couldn't see Nanette Myer doing that. Nanette had to have come to North Avenue for some reason besides gratuitous sex. Sex she could get at any ski resort.

"I'll bet she came down here once or twice to find out what it was like to be a prostitute," she hazarded. "Then she found some other reason for coming. She was a curious person, always asking about people, what they were doing."

Grabowski was issuing orders to Rolondo again. "I want to talk to Lavelle."

Rolondo finished the last bite of his fettuccini and wandered to the doorway. He signaled to someone across the street. By the time Luigi had poured him another glass of iced tea, Lavelle had appeared in the doorway.

She slid her leather-encased hips into the booth. The red leather strained over her belly. St. Clair looked at Grabowski. He was staring at the tight silk blouse over Lavelle's full breasts.

"Miss, uh," Grabowski said. He cleared his throat.

"Call me Lavelle, honey." She arched her back so her breasts stuck out.

Rolondo nudged her. "Ain't no customer, Lavelle. Cop. He wants to know about that white lady that came down here named Mae West. Look at these pictures and see if she's the one you know." He snapped his fingers at St. Clair to pass over the photos, then looked embarrassed.

St. Clair decided to ignore his treating her like a slave. Habits die hard. She passed over the two photos of Nanette and dug more from her purse. They were all taken at the last pool party at the Myer's house. Nanette was wearing flowing black silk pants with a black silk scarf tied around her breasts. She had draped herself over Aaron Simonson, who was sitting in a deck chair looking like he didn't know where to put his hands. The photo had been taken near midnight and the flash lit them like a spotlight. In the fringes of the flash, Nathan Schalz was talking to Virginia Gaust.

Lavelle picked up each photo and peered at them myopically.

"That's her," she said with finality. She tapped the photo of Nanette with the tip of a purple nail. She looked sideways at Rolondo. He picked up the photo and was inspecting it more closely.

"These dudes all doctors?" he asked.

"All but Nanette. I mean Mae West. And the man with all the hair."

"They look drunk."

Grabowski had his notebook out again. "Tell me what went on when you were out on the street with Mae West, Lavelle. What did you do?"

Lavelle slid a quick sideways look at Rolondo. She took a deep breath, drawing Grabowski's eyes again to her chest. "We didn't do nothing different than what we usually do. Mae just walked around with us. She said she was writing a book about being a working girl."

"Did she ever take notes?"

"She never even had a pencil, honey. She just kept this little sequined evening bag with her car keys and a couple dollars."

"No pills?"

"I never seen any. She had some lipstick. She was always putting on lipstick."

"Did she ever buy drugs from anyone?"

"No, sir. She didn't even drink. When we be in a bar, she always ordered sodas. She said she had to drive home."

"So all she did was follow you around all evening?"

"Only a couple hours. She wore these high heels and after a couple hours she'd say her feet were killing her and she'd split in her car."

St. Clair interrupted. "Did she drive home wearing those same clothes?"

"I seen her get into her car once. She put on a long red robe over her clothes, like what you wear at the beach."

"Did she ever go with you on a job, or whatever you call it?"

"You mean with that white dude who wanted two girls? Well, he didn't really want two girls, he wanted her. But I told him, like I told all of them, that she wasn't working, she was waiting for her regular. He wanted to know who her regular was, and she said, 'No one you'd know.' "

"Did she know him?" asked St. Clair.

"I don't think so."

"Then why did she say, 'No one you'd know?' It's an odd thing to say to a total stranger. I'd think she would say,

'Somebody else' or 'My regular,' or something evasive."

Grabowski was scowling at her again. He interrupted. "What happened then, after she said, 'No one you'd know'?"

"The dude said to her, 'If I went with her,' which he meant me, 'would you come along and watch?'"

"He said *that*?" St. Clair burst out.

Grabowski patted her arm. "Let Lavelle tell the story. Get outraged later."

Lavelle was pursing her lips, trying to remember. "She laughed. Then she said, 'Sure! I can't think of nothing I'd rather do.'"

St. Clair mentally corrected the grammer. "So you all went to wherever you go?"

"That's right, honey." Lavelle's eyes slid sideways to Rolondo, who was reaching for a stick of fried zucchini and looking out the window. "And the dude and I went at it and she watched."

"She *watched*!"

Grabowski sighed.

"That's right, honey, I mean Doctor," Lavelle said.

"The whole time?" St. Clair's voice squeaked.

"Well, we didn't get too far, when she cut out. She slammed the door real hard."

"What happened then?"

"The dude laughed. Then he paid me and left."

"Did you ever see him again?"

"He was cruising North Avenue a couple of times, but Mae West wasn't with me."

"You sure it was him?"

"He waved when he went by, honey."

"What about Mae West? When did you see her again?"

"A couple of days later, I guess. She was out with me and some other white dude stopped. This one she knew, because he pulled over, and she got in the car with him, stayed there maybe half an hour, that I seen."

"Did they go anywhere?"

"I don't know. I got busy."

"What time was that?"

"About ten. Couple hours before she took sick."

"Took sick?"

"Went to the hospital. The night Rolondo said he seen her there. I never did figure out how she got there. About eleven-thirty I seen her on the street and a little while later she was gone. I thought she went home, then I heard she went to the hospital and died."

St. Clair picked up the photo of Nanette. "I wish I knew who she sat with in the car the night she died."

"Oh, I can tell you that," Lavelle said. She reached over and took the photo from St. Clair. Laying it carefully on the table, she placed a purple fingernail on the man in the center, the man Nanette had draped herself over. Aaron Simonson.

CHAPTER

12

LAVELLE AND ROLONDO left shortly after, sticking St. Clair with the tab. After the strings of garlic had swayed behind them, Grabowski ordered a cup of coffee. He looked gloomily at her while Luigi splashed coffee into his cup and clattered a dish of spumoni in front of St. Clair. Condensation dripped off the metal cup.

"This silence is more than my nerves can bear," she said, stirring the spumoni. "Let me have it: I should have told you where I was going; I shouldn't be meeting pimps and prostitutes for lunch."

He patted her hand. "Yes, you should have told me where you were going, since it is related to this case, but meeting pimps and prostitutes in delis at noon is not as hazardous as your mother might think."

"And this means I didn't do it!" She gripped his hand. "Aaron Simonson was with Nanette Myer the night she died! He can tell us what Nanette was doing on North Avenue."

"Max, I never thought you killed anyone. It's just that your behavior is making other people wonder."

St. Clair pulled her hand away. "If sleeping with Hank Myer is what you're referring to, Virginia Gaust is doing the same thing, according to you, and you aren't accusing her of murder. She had as ready access to the poison as I did."

Grabowski frowned into his cup. "Forget Dr. Gaust for the moment. I'm wondering if we're seeing a pattern. You learned about Nanette playing the part of Mae West while you were in clinic. That night, somebody attacked you with a ball machine. Did you tell anyone about your discovery?"

"Shirley heard Rolondo telling me, but I didn't mention it to anyone else."

Luigi was standing at the end of the booth, holding the check. St. Clair reached for her purse and pushed the photos toward Luigi. "Do you know this woman?" she demanded, pointing. "When you saw her, she was wearing a red wig."

Luigi pulled wire rims from his apron and took his time looking through the photos. "She was hanging around in front here a couple of times. What did she do, besides the obvious?"

"She got herself killed. What else can you tell me about her?"

Luigi cocked an eyebrow at Grabowski. "This a medical investigation or police business?"

"Go ahead, answer." Grabowski grinned. "Maybe I'll learn how to interrogate people."

Luigi peered again at the photos, then put away his glasses. "She pranced up and down with a couple of Rolondo's girls. Plenty of offers, I'll say that. Once I told her to move along, she was drawing such a crowd."

"Did she ever leave with anyone?"

"I don't watch those hookers every minute. Ask one of the waitresses; they spend more time looking out the window than working."

The waitresses had nothing to add, never saw Nanette Myer. While Grabowski wrote down the names of the weekend help, St. Clair paid the bill. She followed Grabowski out past the redolent garlands of garlic into the hot street.

"Is this what they call legwork?" St. Clair smiled. Heat waves beat against her bare legs. "Who do we talk to now, the weekend waitresses, or Aaron Simonson?"

"*We* talk to no one," Grabowski said, taking her elbow and propelling her toward her car. "*I* talk to these people. You go to work."

"It's only two o'clock. I have an hour before my shift starts."

"Then go home and put ice packs on your face. You're turning the color of an eggplant."

"Let me come, Grabowski. How many reasonably attractive, moderately well-off women plead to follow you around? Can you afford to pass this up?"

"Go home. Or go to St. Agnes and catch up on the paperwork you're always complaining about. Do you want me to call Sergeant Lemie to escort you?"

St. Clair allowed herself to be pushed into her hot car. She scowled at her bruised face in the rearview mirror and unrolled the windows to let the hot street air mingle with the hot car air. An hour and nothing to do. Working in the ER had accustomed her to taking action. Now she couldn't spend even a minute just waiting.

She was staring moodily at two prostitutes climbing into an air-conditioned white Impala when her eye fell upon the dilapidated brick of the North Avenue Public Health Clinic. Kareena Singh was in there, she remembered. Kareena doctored everyone in the neighborhood, resident or transient. She might have heard something about Nanette Myer, a.k.a. Mae West. Also, the district public health nurses who worked out of that clinic knew the neighborhoods even better than the cops on drug detail. They might have noticed something.

St. Clair rolled up her windows again. Keeping an eye out for Grabowski's unmarked squad car, she dodged across the traffic ripping down North Avenue and followed a nurse up the marble steps of the clinic.

Inside, it was cool. The building was originally a butcher shop, and the walls were of white tile to the fourteen-foot ceiling. A wooden ceiling fan stirred the air above the partitions. A protesting baby was getting a shot.

Kareena was sitting at her desk reading a medical journal and sipping iced tea. She was wearing a salmon-colored sari with gold threads woven through it, and was dabbing her face with a scented wet handkerchief. She raised a quiet hand in greeting.

"I hear you're suspected of poisoning Hank Myer's wife,"

she said, a small smile on her dark face.

"News travels fast. How do you know?"

"One of the public health nurses drove a girl over to St. Agnes ER yesterday and hung around to hear the gossip."

"What else did she hear?"

"That before you started working at St. Agnes, you used the poison as a research drug; that you were covering the ER when Mrs. Myer came in; and that she came in dressed up like a prostitute."

"All true." St. Clair fanned herself with the medical journal. Sweat had broken out on her face at the thought that her supposed midnight tryst with Hank Myer might also be public knowledge.

"Why would anyone want to kill Nanette Myer?" Kareena asked.

"I wish I knew. I don't even know where the poison came from. Without that information, I can't begin to figure out who poisoned her." St. Clair slumped in the wooden chair.

Dr. Singh smiled. "Is this a one-woman investigation? Aren't the police looking into this?"

"They aren't coming up with anything, and I'm wondering if they're looking in the right place. I think we should be searching for the people Nanette was with in the inner city. The police are only interviewing her friends."

"Could one of her friends have killed her?"

St. Clair frowned. "Because of the short time it takes for tetrodotoxin to take effect, she had to have been poisoned while she was in the inner city. What would her friends be doing there?"

Dr. Singh raised an eyebrow. "The question is, what was Mrs. Myer doing in the inner city?"

St. Clair lowered her voice. There were no walls in these storefront clinics, just sheets pinned to wooden frames. "Did you ever hear of a prostitute who called herself Mae West?"

Dr. Singh fanned herself. "A woman by that name came into evening clinic once. She was wearing a red wig. I remember because after she left, the nurses joked about the name."

"Why did she come in?"

"Cut knee. She was wearing absurdly high heels, and she fell on the sidewalk. Why?"

"That was Nanette Myer. She used to dress up like a prostitute and parade up and down North Avenue."

"You're joking."

"She said she was writing a book on prostitution, but nobody ever saw her take notes. All I know is she was dressed like a prostitute the night she died, and the taxi that brought her picked her up right near here, on Twenty-first and North."

"Did Mrs. Myer ever actually pick up men?"

"She left with a different man on two separate occasions, but I'm convinced she knew them."

A circle of nurses had gathered at the opening of the partition. Despite Maxene's efforts to keep the conversation confidential, everyone had overheard.

"Have any of you ever seen that prostitute named Mae West when she was out on the street?" Kareena asked. No one had.

"Ask the other nurses," St. Clair said. "Especially the nurses who cover Twenty-first and North. The Elm Elementary School nurse, the district nurses, anybody on special projects. I need to know anything about her, like what she was doing the Sunday after the Fourth."

It was 2:30 when St. Clair left the clinic. She walked the block down to Twenty-first and North and stood on the corner. The dust and exhaust fumes made her sneeze. The intersection was little different than other North Avenue intersections. On one corner stood a dusty grocery with a few dilapidated vegetables in boxes in the window. Across the street was a boarded-up drugstore. On the other corner was an apartment building with empty vodka bottles by the front door. The final corner was an empty lot.

Grabowski had said the taxi picked up Nanette near Elm Elementary School, St. Clair remembered, looking around

her. That meant down the block away from the noisy intersection, nearer the grocery or the apartment building. She
walked slowly around the corner of the grocery. The side
door on Twenty-first opened to a dusty flight of stairs. She
banged on the partially open door. No answer. At the top
of the stairs was nothing, an empty room.

Between the grocery and the school stood a row of
dilapidated Milwaukee bungalows with sagging porches
and broken windows. A filthy dog, staked by a rope in one
yard, scratched himself and whined at her. St. Clair jotted
down the addresses so she could call the North Avenue
Clinic and find out which district nurse covered the area.
Nurses kept files on every family in the city—even knew
where they moved.

The apartment building seemed more promising, or at
least more occupied. Laundry hung out most windows. St.
Clair crossed the street and tried the front door. Locked. She
made a note of the address and walked back to her car.

It was nearly 3:00 P.M. when she got to St. Agnes'. She
hurried into the ER, noticed no patients had arrived yet, and
ran down the steps to Pathology to see if Aaron Simonson
had talked to Grabowski yet. The double doors to the lab
were locked and the shades pulled over the door windows.
A sliver of light shone between the doors. St. Clair put her
mouth to the crack.

"Aaron, it's me, Maxene. Let me in."

After a minute, the locked door clicked open and
Simonson let her push through. He locked the door behind
her and began pulling on a new set of surgical gloves.

"Can't a person work in peace?" he snarled, turning his
attention to the body lying on the exam table. Simonson's
puffy eyes were bloodshot, and his plump cheeks had a
day's growth of beard. "I've got so many cadavers stacked
up here, I feel like Dracula."

"Sister Rosalie on you again?"

"Like the Grand Inquisitor. I locked the door to keep her
out."

"Then you haven't talked to Detective Grabowski yet."

"Who?" He flipped what looked like a liver into a pan. St. Clair averted her eyes.

"The detective who was here a few days ago with Nanette Myer's blood results."

"I haven't talked to anybody. Nobody knows I'm here, and that's the way I want to keep it. Say, what happened to you?" He finally looked up from the body cavity he was fishing around in to notice her bruised face.

"I was at the tennis club, and somebody turned on a ball machine when I was standing in front of it."

"Not your partner, I hope." He chuckled.

"I never saw the person."

"An odd accident."

"It could be a deliberate attack. I think I've discovered something about Nanette Myer's killer. The person may be trying to stop me from getting any further."

Simonson kept poking at the cadaver. "With a ball machine? Get serious. But what have you found out?" He slid a new blade onto his scalpel.

"Two things, and you already know them," St. Clair said evenly. "First, Nanette Myer used to dress up like a prostitute and stand around on North Avenue."

The scalpel clattered to the floor.

"I also know that you met Nanette on North Avenue and she got into your car." Maxene paused. "Isn't it time you told me what happened to Nanette that night?"

Simonson looked at his hand. The falling scalpel had nicked his finger and blood was seeping under the rubber glove. He stripped off both gloves and tossed them into the garbage. Then he started scrubbing his hands at the sink, the green liquid soap foaming into reddish bubbles.

"Aaron," St. Clair persisted. "Tell me what really happened that night."

"I don't know. I wasn't there." He dried his hands and opened a new pack of surgical gloves.

"A prostitute who came into the ER identified you from a photo," St. Clair said.

He looked up sharply. "What photo? Where did she get it?"

"I showed it to her." This wasn't how St. Clair had pictured the confrontation. Aaron was supposed to crumble, admit his guilt, then confess he killed Nanette Myer or give a good reason why he hadn't. He wasn't supposed to be interrogating Maxene.

"Where did you get it?" he demanded.

"Were you there, Aaron, or weren't you?"

"I wasn't. I didn't know Nanette was parading around as a prostitute, and I didn't meet her on North Avenue."

St. Clair's argument was cut off by the blare of the paging system. "Dr. St. Clair to the ER," nasaled the operator. St. Clair stalked out, smacking the heavy wooden doors behind her.

CHAPTER

13

AT 11:45, THE ER was empty. Dr. St. Clair felt exhausted. Her head ached, her swollen face throbbed, and she was seeing flashing lights, probably a migraine caused by the head trauma. Dr. Malech, her midnight replacement, arrived early, and, after one look at her face, ordered her home. St. Clair let the security guard walk her to her car, and she drove home with the windows down to let the soft night air cool her aching face.

The breeze revived her. As she drove across the Locust Street bridge into the cooler lakeside suburbs, the air freshened, and the scent of flowers and wet grass mixed with the heavier street smells. A few blocks from her apartment, she pulled into an all-night grocery for milk and bread. The long red hotdog revolving on the shiny greased grill looked appetizing. Bad for the digestion but good for the soul. She bought one and took a few bites in the car, finishing it as she walked up the dark stairs to her apartment. At the top, she tossed the last salty morsel into her mouth and licked the ketchup off her fingers.

The attacker caught her standing there, fingers in her mouth. He lunged out of the darkness, a heavy, sweaty nightmare. Hot breath panted against the back of her neck and a strong hand crushed over her mouth. She clawed at the fingers, but a wire quickly rounded her neck, and the hands yanked it tight around her throat.

"Help!" she screamed. The wire had caught her with her fingers in her mouth and lashed her wrist tightly against

107

her throat, choking her. The wire cut deep into her arm. She screamed in pain and lashed backward with her other elbow, as she had been taught in the self-defense course at St. Agnes. The hand around her face loosened.

"Help!" she screamed again, hoping her downstairs neighbor was home and not in a drunken stupor.

"Maxene! I'm coming!" she heard him shout, and his feet pounded toward the back stairs that led up to her kitchen. Was the kitchen door locked? It couldn't be. She always forgot to lock inside doors. She heard the door bang open and the clatter of her rescuer falling over the kitchen table.

For an instant, the pressure on the wire slackened and she forced it away from her, her arm already numb. She fell to the floor, only faintly aware of feet pounding down the front stairs. When her neighbor turned on the light, she was sobbing uncontrollably in a pool of blood, a coil of picture wire loose around her throat.

Detective Grabowski met her and the Aid Unit at the entrance to St. Agnes ER. His face was devoid of expression, but his hand shook when he gripped her shoulder, and she felt the hard muscles of his clenched jaw when he bent over the stretcher to press his face against hers.

"I should have driven you home, Max. After one attack, I knew this might happen. I'll never forgive myself."

"Not your fault, Grabowski." Loss of blood was making her woozy. Her mouth felt dry, and her tongue too big. She groped for his hand. He held it tightly, his fingers slipping on the blood still wet between her fingers.

"What happened, Max? Can you talk now?"

"Somebody was waiting in my apartment. He tried to choke me with a wire, but he got the wire around my arm, too. I was eating a hotdog." She giggled, shock taking over.

The ER nurse slid a blood pressure cuff around her good arm. The cuff tightened, then loosened. St. Clair felt the dull pain of a needle jab into the vein on the inside of her elbow. A plastic IV bag appeared in the rack over her head.

It swung gently. The stretcher began to move.

"Surgery time," Dr. Malech's cheery voice said. "Interrogate the victim later."

St. Clair closed her eyes. She felt Grabowski's lips on her forehead.

She woke up in a hospital bed. It was daylight, and pigeons were strutting along the ledge outside her window. Their shiny black eyes glittered. For a moment she couldn't remember where she was, then the sight of Sergeant Lemie sitting solidly in the visitor's chair brought it all back. She stretched her legs and arms. They were still stiff from the balls hitting her. But her right arm didn't move. It was splinted elbow to fingers, the splint held in place with an Ace wrap.

Sergeant Lemie looked up from her book. "I'm instructed to tell you not to wiggle your fingers," she said. "Something about muscle repair. How are you feeling?"

"Like I've been eating cotton balls."

"Can you remember anything more about what happened? Grabowski will be in to talk to you soon."

Grabowski arrived half an hour later, pushing his way into the room behind a huge floral offering.

"You shouldn't have!" St. Clair smiled.

"I didn't. These are from your cohorts in the ER. This is from me," and he handed her a small bouquet of violets, cool and fragrant against her cheek.

He settled in the visitor's chair and pulled out a notebook. "Tell me everything from the moment you left your car until the ambulance arrived."

St. Clair did, adding extras, such as her afternoon conversations with Kareena Singh and Aaron Simonson, and her trip to Twenty-first and North Avenue.

"Big coincidence. Simonson finds out you know he picked up the murdered woman a few hours before she died, and ten hours later someone tries to strangle you. Follows the same pattern as the ball accident."

"Aaron couldn't strangle anyone. He might hurt his hands."

"I'll decide that when I find him. No one's seen him except you. The pathology lab is locked, and he isn't home. The hospital switchboard says he hasn't punched in for two days."

"Then he's still in his lab. He locks the door and works nonstop when he gets behind. He even sleeps in there next to the cadavers. He's hiding from Sister Rosalie."

"But not from me." The door swished behind him as he left. St. Clair slept.

Hospitals are no place to go when you need rest, St. Clair decided. "The noise here makes an elementary school sound quiet," St. Clair complained to Hank Myer, who stopped by at noon during hospital rounds. "Nurses talk loudly, the intercom wakes me up every time I get to sleep, my room-mates are wheeled in and out at all hours, phones ring, doctors make rounds. Get me out of here. I need some rest."

He gave her a quick kiss on the cheek. "I read your chart; you've had quite an accident. Two of them, I hear." He touched the bruise on her cheek. "It isn't safe for a single woman to work nights and go home to an empty apartment. Why don't you quit the ER and go back to research?"

"These aren't random muggings, Hank. I've figured out something about Nanette's death. Something someone doesn't want me to know. If only I knew what it was."

Myer stood up abruptly and paced around the room. "Stop this silly business, Maxene. You're a doctor, not a detective. If the police can't turn up anything, how can you? You're getting yourself hurt."

"But don't you see what that means? I'm making some-one nervous! I'm getting close!"

"Stop it, Maxene!" He put his hand on the door handle. "Nanette is dead. Let her stay dead."

The door closed before she could answer.

St. Clair languished in bed the rest of the afternoon. She drifted in and out of a doze, watching blocks of sun move across the floor. Grabowski called at six, saying he was on his way over. Soon after, the surgical resident appeared and said Maxene could go home. He sprawled in her visitor's chair and wrote her discharge note, eating his dinner from a patient's tray marked "Room 614."

"Room six-fourteen sleeping through dinner?" St. Clair moved stiffly to the tiny bathroom to change into the green scrub suit the resident had brought at her request. Her own clothes were so horribly bloodstained she had stuffed them into the wastebasket.

"Room six-fourteen died," the resident said. "We keep ordering his meals until food service notices he's not on the patient roster. Free food."

St. Clair ate her own dinner and watched the pigeons until Grabowski arrived to take her home. He had parked in the no-parking zone near the front door. The car smelled of fried fish. She pushed the food wrappers away with her foot and closed her eyes. "I'm going to live on deli-delivered food until I feel like getting up," she murmured.

After a few minutes she opened her eyes to see Lake Michigan spread out in front of her. The car was turning onto the short elevated freeway that led to the south side.

"Wrong turn," she mumbled. "I live north, not south."

"We're going to my house. I'm not letting you get beat up a third time."

"You have a special guest room for hiding victims?"

"No, damn it." He hit the heel of his hand against the steering wheel. "Every time I leave you alone, you get hurt. Isn't sewing up the victims of the world enough for you? Do you have to become a victim yourself?"

The freeway ended, and he jerked the car to a stop on a side street. He put his arms around her. "Don't cry, Max. Everytime you get beat up, it scares me."

She snuffled into his shirt. "Thanks for taking care of me, Grabowski. I'm not used to that. I forget to tell you thanks. But I don't feel good. I want to sleep for a week."

She drifted off to sleep, the dregs of yesterday's anesthesia dragging down her tired brain. She was only dimly aware of the car moving again, stopping again, and of her own stumbling feet across a wooden porch and into a cool and shaded bedroom.

CHAPTER

14

SQUAWKING GULLS WOKE her. St. Clair stared at the clock, trying to decide whether 8:00 meant morning or evening. Grabowski's closet door stood open to show an uneven row of shirts. Papers were piled on the dresser, and book and magazines lay in an unsymmetrical jumble on the night table. Hank Myer's interior designer would faint in this house, Maxene decided. It looked like the resident had moved in with as few possessions as possible and could move out again the same way. The thought saddened her unaccountably, and she swung her legs stiffly out of bed to go in search of the tenant.

She found him sitting at the kitchen table, wearing purple running shorts and a T-shirt, his nose buried in the sports page. The newspaper lowered.

"Get enough sleep?"

"Feels like it. Is this morning or evening?"

"Morning. We have the whole day ahead of us."

"Don't you have work to do?"

"My chief suspect is right here. Besides, it's Sunday."

He shuffled the papers into a pile and stood up to pour coffee.

"What happened while I was asleep?" she yawned, sinking into a chair. "Did you ever catch up with Aaron Simonson?"

"Found him in the hospital cafeteria poisoning himself on fish sticks."

"Did he admit he was Nanette Myer's secret encounter?"

"Yes and no. He admitted he knew she was parading around North Avenue, and he admitted he picked her up

112

in his car the night she was killed, but he never admitted to being a customer or a murderer."

"What did he do when he picked her up?"

"That's where his story gets shaky. He claims he took her home."

"But she was back on North Avenue when the taxi picked her up."

"He says he doesn't know how she got there, that he told her what she was doing was insane, and he took her home."

St. Clair sipped the coffee. "That sounds like Aaron. He is used to being the authority in his work, and he would immediately decide the best thing for her. He'd bundle her into his car and drive her home."

"Look at the situation objectively, Maxene. You're trying to turn facts around so Simonson couldn't have done it."

"Aaron isn't the type to take the risks a murderer takes. Aaron is a pathologist. His work is as defined as you can get and still be a doctor. He deals with bits of information analyzed by lab tests. He doesn't deal with people . . . he wouldn't know how."

"Using personality analysis to help find murderers is skating on thin ice. All kinds of people become murderers when they're faced with a situation they can't resolve. Especially people who can't deal with people."

"I think something went on between him and Nanette that could be tied up with why he went to North Avenue to see her. Here, look at this photo again." She unstuck her purse from the syrupy counter.

"See?" she pointed. "They're both smiling, but look at the grip she has on his arm. He's trying to pull away. And look at the expression on Hank's face in the background. Laughing, but not a nice smile. He's got his eyes right on them. I think they were having an affair, and Aaron wanted out."

"Take a deep breath, Max. Aaron Simonson was married once, something I turned up after a few hours on the phone. He was married and divorced in Chicago. His wife's name was Nanette. Later, Nanette Myer." Grabowski grinned at her expression. "What does that do to your theory about an affair?"

St. Clair took a minute to digest this. "They could still have been having an affair," she said stubbornly. "It's easier to love someone when you're not married to the person. Aaron probably found out Nanette was traipsing around North Avenue and decided to bring her home, in a husbandlike way."

"Look at the facts, Maxene. Simonson admits to putting her in his car just a few hours before she died. He could have slipped her the poison in a breath mint. He could have stolen the toxin out of your unlocked and unguarded refrigerator. He could have set the ball machine on you and tried to strangle you in your apartment. He has no alibis for any time, just claims he was working in the lab. How I can prove all this, I don't know, but I'll have my eye on him from now on. I don't think he'll attack you again, though. Everything you know, I also know."

He picked up a pair of running shoes and a sack of sweet rolls off the counter. "Bring your coffee outside. Fresh air is good for wounded people."

The air smelled of roses and mown grass. Gulls drifted over the beach in lazy circles, harsh cries echoing the shouts of children. A string of grackles swung on the telephone line. Someone was frying bacon. St. Clair sipped her coffee and watched Grabowski lace his running shoes. His muscular legs looked like the kind to snuggle up against on cold winter nights, she decided. She sank into a deck chair and propped her own legs on the wooden porch railing. Across the road, Lake Michigan stretched flat and serene, a calm blue mirror of the sky, so close in color it was impossible to say where water ended and sky began. A tiny freighter perched precariously on the invisible horizon, then disappeared.

She watched Grabowski lope down the bike path along the beach and around the curve. Silver blue water lapped gently. A long bone of driftwood, sunbleached to silver gray, shone like a thin moon. She fastened her eyes on the haze that was horizon and tried to put her thoughts in order. What did she know? She must have some fact in her possession that was causing someone to want her dead. Perhaps Nanette Myer had said something before she died that might point to the person who killed her.

She closed her eyes and focused on the night Nanette died. Nanette said her husband was out of town. She said she had never had these symptoms before. She said she thought it was an antibiotic, whatever "it" was.

That was all. Maxene hadn't even seen the body after the attempt to revive her had failed. But Aaron had. Maybe he found out something from the autopsy he hadn't written in the report. Then why wasn't the murderer trying to strangle him? She needed to talk to Aaron again, to go over every detail of that autopsy.

A car door slammed. Quiet footsteps were crossing the grass toward her. Panic flooded her. Not again! Not in broad daylight! She jerked open her eyes. Hank Myer was standing at the foot of the steps.

"What are you doing here?" he said, taking in the small bungalow with its peeling paint, the kitchen chair on the porch, the chipped mug of coffee.

"How did you know where I was?"

"I asked at the nurse's station. The whole hospital knows you're recuperating in this Polack stronghold."

Hank seated himself carefully on the creaking porch steps. He outweighed Grabowski by fifty pounds, St. Clair estimated. Tennis legs. She'd seen him playing tennis with Virginia once or twice, or hitting against the ball machine.

"Any more of that coffee?"

"In the kitchen."

He returned with a chipped mug of water. "Quite the homemaker, your detective. Does he live on beer?"

"Lend him your housekeeper."

"I'm not criticizing, just commenting. Where did you sleep last night? Surely not on the couch. So middle class."

"Do I ask where you sleep every night?"

The remark slid away on the breeze. "You're referring to

Virginia, I suppose. Do you mind?" He sounded worried.

"Not in the least."

They watched the flock of grackles drop onto the grass from the telephone wire. They poked their heavy beaks into the soil.

"Aaron Simonson told me you think he had something to do with my wife's death," Myer said.

"Did he tell you why?"

"You tell me. I need to know what you found out about Nanette."

"You mean what she did with her spare time?" They were sparring, circling, like the grackles on the lawn.

"I know what Nanette was doing on North Avenue, if that's what you mean by 'her spare time.' I've known from the beginning. The little nymphomaniac started acting even more peculiar than usual, so I had her followed by a detective. A private one."

His grim features told her how he felt. St. Clair forced herself to ask the next question. "Did the detective ever see her actually leave with someone?"

"You mean, did she ever pick up anyone? No." He sighed. "The detective even pretended to be a customer, and she wouldn't go for it. Why not, I don't know. She slept with anyone else who lifted an eyebrow at her."

"Like Aaron Simonson."

He didn't answer.

"Hank, what was she doing on North Avenue?"

He lifted his hands. "How the hell should I know? She was nuts. She was bored. She was curious. She was always doing crazy things like that. I told her to get a job to fill up her time, but she was having too much fun jetting here and there— skiing vacations, Bahamas, anywhere she wanted to go. She had to go down to North Avenue and get more fun there."

"That makes sense, Hank, if she only went once or twice. But she went back at least four times. What was the purpose? The question of how prostitutes are victimized can be answered in a few minutes."

He didn't answer.

"Did she ever talk to you about why she went there?"

Hank put his head in his hands. "She used to talk about the difference between feeling like a victim versus being one. She said that all her married life, she felt like a victim of the medical system—a victim of my schedule, or the phone. She said all people felt like victims when they were around doctors. She said she went to North Avenue to find out how real victims lived. I guess she thought she could get it out of her system. She was nuts."

Grabowski had finished his run and was panting toward them across the lawn. His dark hair dripped with perspiration. His running shorts hung loose on his hipbones. Hank, cool in khaki shorts and a white knit shirt, looked him over.

"I hear you've been finding out unsavory things about my dead wife."

"We're trying to find out how she died. Finding out what she was doing at the time was an unfortunate side effect, as you might say in your profession." Grabowski was catching his breath. "Murder investigations have a way of turning up facts people would rather not know."

"I suppose you think I killed her. Aren't husbands the first to be suspected?"

Maxene gasped.

Grabowski smiled thinly.

"Only husbands whose wives' behavior has exceeded societal bounds."

Behind him, the beach was filling up with people. Two lifeguards, blond and husky, wearing red shorts and dark glasses, were dragging a cooler between them to the lifeguard chair. A third lifeguard unhitched a rowboat from a piling and hauled it through the sand toward the water. The oars bounced hollowly. A swarm of children on bicycles pedalled madly on the bike path, shrill laughter floating over the sand. At the bike stand, they lit, gull-like, and pulled chains through their tires, then pranced off carrying bright towels.

Grabowski was sweating profusely, exertion having caught up with him. Rivers of sweat ran down his forehead. He blinked it out of his eyes. "I'm going to cool off," he said abruptly. He walked across the street toward the water, every muscle visible under his sweat-soaked shirt and nylon shorts. At the edge of the sun-spotted water, he pulled off his running shoes, walked steadily into the lake, waded up to his thighs, then dove. His head surfaced, sleek against the light. He started a slow crawl.

"How does Superman stand that frigid water?" Myer said. "Ice is still floating at the headwaters."

"Shut up." St. Clair started to stand, but Myer's hand closed around her wrist. He pulled her down.

"Maxene, why are you staying here with that Polack cop?"

"For my own protection, and because I want to."

"And because you're still trying to prove my wife died because someone poisoned her, and you think that Polack will help you."

"Afraid of what I might find?"

"Certainly not. You think I resorted to poisoning my wife just to straighten out her behavior? Anybody could have poisoned her, anytime. You yourself could have kept a vial of that stuff at your apartment and met Nanette somewhere for a drink. It's easy to doctor someone's drink when they're looking the other way."

St. Clair gaped at him. "What are you talking about? I didn't kill her. Why should I? I barely knew her."

Myer shrugged. "I'm just making a point. If you have the means, which you did, the method is easy when you're talking about poison."

"But why should I kill her?" St. Clair's voice shook.

Myer didn't seem to notice. "Nanette and I had been falling apart for a long time. She wanted a different husband than me, wanted to be something more than she was. She said that doctors had so much power of position that being married to one was repressive. She said she felt like a fifth wheel; that every time I came into a room, she became invisible. People stopped talking to her and started talking to me. She hated doctor parties because she said doctors talked to doctors and ignored everyone else. She said the only reason she had affairs was to prove she was an actual living person."

St. Clair tried to concentrate on what he was saying. "She gave a lot of doctor parties at your house, at restaurants. Why, if she hated doctors so much?"

Hank shrugged. "Doctors are the people we know."

"Do you think that her going to North Avenue had something to do with how she felt about being a doctor's wife?"

"I don't know why she went to North Avenue. But after she started going there, she acted differently. She dropped in on poor Aaron at his house and forced herself on him. She started getting up early in the mornings; she called people up to arrange lunches, dinners. She called Virginia to play tennis, for God's sake. They barely knew each other."

Myer let go of her wrist and took her hand. "We're alike, you and I. I need you now, like you needed me during your divorce. I need companionship and sympathy. I need love. I need you. Call me when you decide to get out of this place. There's a place in my house for you." He strode across the lawn to his car.

Her wrist was sore where his heavy fingers had dug into the flesh. She rubbed it and watched his car vanish around the corner. She felt, rather than saw, Grabowski sink into the chair Myer had just vacated.

"What did he want?"

She didn't trust her voice. "Companionship, mostly. But also, he thinks I actually could have killed his wife!"

A long silence. "Why would he say that?"

"The poison came from my lab, and I knew her well enough to administer it."

"But why would you do it?"

"He didn't say. He already knew what his wife was doing on North Avenue. He had her followed by a detective. And he knew that Aaron Simonson knew she was out on North Avenue." She forced the rest of what Hank had said out of her mind.

Grabowski pulled off his wet shirt and flung it over the rail. "According to Lavelle, Nanette only talked to two men while she was hanging around North Avenue. One she left with in a car the night she died. That was Aaron Simonson. The other she watched have sex with Lavelle. Could that person have been Dr. Myer?"

The idea hit her like a splash of icy lake water. "It could have been the detective Hank hired."

"Not the detective. I talked to him yesterday."

"Then it was somebody else, Grabowski. We have to spread more pictures around, see if Lavelle's friends recognize anybody else."

"You sound desperate, Maxene. Face it. Her murderer came from her own circle, and it could have been Myer or Simonson."

A hot wind was blowing across her legs. The day would be a scorcher. Grabowski poked a cold beer at her. She shook her head absently.

"Relax," Grabowski said, opening the beer for himself. "We're already leafletting the inner city with photos of all Nanette's close male acquaintances. You still have hope."

"I thought nobody there talks to cops."

"What other way is there?"

"Let me try, Grabowski. I found Rolondo, didn't I? I discovered it was Aaron who picked up Nanette that night."

Grabowski rolled his beer across his forehead. "It's so far outside regulations, I don't even want to think about it. On the other hand, it might just work."

"Let me see the photos you were planning to pass around."

She watched him walk to his car across the stubbly dry lawn. Dessicated daisies poked up in the border. St. Clair started imagining what the front garden would be like filled with summer flowers. But planting flowers smacked of permanence, she thought. This little house was as permanent as that small white cloud scudding across the sky.

Grabowski dropped a manila envelope in her lap. Inside were photos of all the doctors she knew, glossy posed shots taken from the medical society directory.

"No one will recognize these, Grabowski. I barely recognize them myself, and I know these people."

"You have a better idea?"

"Sure. I have a whole mess of candid photos at my flat that I took at those endless doctor parties. Pass those around."

"You always carry a camera?"

"It's my only hobby. I keep it up to pretend the life I lead is normal."

After Grabowski showered and changed into another pair of running shorts, he drove her across town to her place. His car still reeked of take-out fried fish. No cars were parked next to her cracked and lumpy sidewalk, but Grabowski insisted on going up first to test for intruders. She waited in the car, perspiring from nervousness as well as heat. She hadn't noticed Grabowski wearing a gun, although it was police regulations that all off-duty police carry their weapon. Maybe the gun was in the car with her. At last, the door to her little balcony opened, and Grabowski waved her up.

The rooms were hot and airless. A faint hot breeze stirred the papers she had left on the table. It took only a few minutes to stuff some clothes from her minimal collection into a suitcase. When she came back to the kitchen, Grabowski was holding a case of Miller beer under one arm and pouring spoiled milk down the sink with the other.

"Where are the photos?" he demanded. "I hope they haven't all melted. It's too hot to live in an upper apartment."

She pulled out a kitchen drawer and pointed to the carefully organized rows of photos and negatives. Grabowski stuck the entire drawer under his other arm.

By the time they returned to Grabowski's little blue-shuttered bungalow, sleep was dragging down St. Clair's eyelids. Being attacked and suffering the manipulations of the emergency room take a toll on a body, St. Clair reminded herself. She always told her patients to take time

to hide in a quiet place and sleep off the trauma. It was drifting through her mind to tell Rolondo to give his ladies a day
off after they had spent time in the ER, when she fell
asleep.

She woke late in the afternoon, groggy but refreshed.
Grabowski was sitting in his usual porch chair, a pile of
empty beer cans at his feet, the cooler within arm's reach.
He was working his way through a stack of reports that
spilled out of a box. He handed her a bottle of Miller.

"I've been going through your photos," he said, gesturing
to a shoebox on top of the kitchen drawer that was propped
on the railing. "I've found some we can use."

She settled into a chair and pulled the shoebox into
her lap. On the top lay a small pile of photos. One she
recognized as a near duplicate of the photo she had originally shown Lavelle of Aaron Simonson and Nanette at
the party. There were more from that party—a closeup of
Hank, laughing into the camera, a clear shot of him chatting
with Virginia Gaust. Nathan was in the background, leering
drunkenly. There were some from way back: a shot of
herself with Alan. She shuddered at this piece of her past.
The rumors she had ground out of her memory during her
divorce surged back, like waves. Alan and Virginia, Alan
and the lab tech, Alan and a student nurse. God! Who hadn't
the man slept with? She had filed for divorce even before
she heard all the rumors.

Grabowski touched her arm. "What are you thinking
about that's causing such deep breathing?"

"I was remembering something I heard about my ex-
husband and Dr. Gaust.

"Oh." Grabowski looked out over the blue lake.

"You heard all the rumors from the doctors' wives, I
suppose."

"It came up, yes. But I heard them while you were
going through your divorce. The nurses in the ER noticed
that you cheered up after you went out with me, so they
kept feeding me information about you, hoping I'd stay
interested."

"What else did these lively gossips tell you? Was Alan sleeping with anyone else?"

Grabowski was silent. The answer dropped neatly into her mind.

"Nanette."

CHAPTER

15

BY 3:00 TUESDAY afternoon, St. Clair was ready to go back to work. Her right arm was bandaged wrist to elbow, and she still had one black eye, but both hands were functional. A second night's uninterrupted sleep in Grabowski's quiet bedroom, plus daily naps and a few cleansing, leisurely walks down the beach had turned her into a new woman.

The ER was deserted when she walked in, mid-afternoon lull before the rush-hour traffic accidents and after-school bicycle collisions. Shirley and Joella were at the nurse's station charging up their batteries with a box of chocolates. The card read "Maxene" she noticed. From Aaron Simonson.

"Not like Aaron," St. Clair said, biting into a caramel. She was struck suddenly by how easy it would be to poison a box of chocolates.

"He's never sent candy to anybody in the hospital," Joella agreed. "Or flowers. Even the morning after."

The ER doors opened and two medics wheeled in a woman with a bleeding face, the first accident victim of the night. Rolondo the pimp brought in the twentieth victim. It was Lavelle, her lip split open again along the suture line.

"She'll need plastic surgery this time," St. Clair told Rolondo. "Once a partially healed wound is reopened, it won't heal smoothly unless it's excised and restitched by a plastic surgeon." She drew Rolondo toward the admitting desk, away from Lavelle's hearing. "How valuable is Lavelle to you?" she asked.

Rolondo had spotted the box of chocolates on the desk. He poked some until he found a cream, then dropped the wrapper on the floor. "Lavelle used to be one of my best—a real producer—but she dropped off. Says she's tired. She's getting old, is what she is."

"She's been beaten up too many times, Rolondo. She needs a long time to recover from this one."

"How much this going to cost me?"

"With plastic surgery and a night in the hospital, about twenty-five hundred dollars. And welfare won't cover the plastic surgery."

"What if you sew her up in the ER?"

"The same as usual—about four hundred. Welfare will cover part. But her mouth won't heal straight. There could be nerve damage that my surgical skills can't compensate for."

"She ain't no good to me without no face."

St. Clair waited while Rolondo rummaged through the chocolates.

"Tell you what, Doc," he said. "I'll give her a choice. For twenty-five hundred, she gets a new face, and she stays in the hospital two or three days. Then she comes back to work. For four hundred, welfare pays, and she can quit. She's always whining about going back to Alabama. She's got at least ten thousand dollars stashed in banks all over town so she can start up some little chicken farm there. She thinks I don't know. Little I don't know. Like where she gets her extra cash."

He brushed past her toward the curtained area where Lavelle waited.

Joella stopped punching the keys of her computer and reached for the box of chocolates.

"Some choice that girl got. Working for him got her beat up; he should pay to fix her. And he ate all the creams."

St. Clair picked up the next chart and started toward another occupied exam table. She would let Rolondo have a few minutes with his employee, but the outcome was predictable.

"Joella," she said. "Find out if there's a plastic surgeon in the house who won't mind looking over my shoulder while I try to be a plastic surgeon."

Maxene stopped Rolondo as he was walking out the door. She handed him the packet of photos. "Do you recognize anyone?" she asked.

"Didn't I see these before?" He glanced at the top one, then at the fifty cc syringe on the tray that Shirley was wheeling toward Lavelle's cubicle. He took the photos and left.

"I hear you're going back to Alabama," St. Clair said to Lavelle, who was buried under a carefully layered set of sterile towels. Only her lacerated lip was visible.

"You heard right." The lip barely moved but the message was clear. "I had enough of men to last me a lifetime."

St. Clair leaned her hip against the exam table and waited for the numbness to take over Lavelle's face. "Rolondo said you get extra cash from somewhere."

"He can't stop me."

"If you're selling blood, wait a couple months. Let yourself heal."

"Don't talk," Shirley said, handing St. Clair a curved needle with suture attached. The fine nylon thread trailed through the air like a cobweb.

By the time St. Clair had finished, a pink telephone message slip was waiting for her. Grabowski wanted her to call.

"There's nothing new," he said. "I'm just checking to make sure you aren't planning anything rash."

St. Clair hung up feeling there was something she should be telling him, but not sure what it was. Joella handed her another message slip. It was from Rolondo. "Saturday, same place," it read.

"Luigi's Italian Deli on North Avenue," St. Clair promptly explained to Joella. No point in letting rumors fly all over the hospital. "Sometimes he's in there when I'm having lunch with Dr. Singh."

St. Clair wondered if Rolondo was really going to show the photos around or just throw them out. They weren't exactly evidence, and Grabowski had copies, but one never knew what the Rolondos of the world would do, given an advantage.

She wrote out post-surgical instructions for Lavelle—how to ice the wound, how to keep it clean. "Get plenty of rest—alone," she said. "No going out and making extra cash. The sooner you get out of Milwaukee, the better."

Lavelle agreed, to the point of refusing to stay in the hospital overnight. She asked for a taxi to take her home. A friend could give her a ride as far as Chicago that very night, she said. She wanted to be out of town before Rolondo changed his mind.

The ER was empty by the time Lavelle's cab arrived. St. Clair walked outside with her. The warm, muggy air smelled sweet after the air-conditioned sterility of the ER. Even the smells of exhaust fumes and fried cabbage were pleasant.

"Stay out of hospitals," St. Clair said, giving Lavelle's shoulder an affectionate pat. "I'm going to miss you. If you're ever back in town, look me up. We'll go to Luigi's, if I'm not in prison on a murder charge."

"They really think you killed Mae West?" Lavelle mumbled, sounding worried.

"I don't know." Maxene felt unconvinced. "The police have a couple other suspects, but I don't think they have the right ones. The problem is that nobody had any reason to kill Nanette. She was having a brief affair with my husband before our divorce, which makes some people point at me, but if I went after everyone who slept with my ex-husband, I'd be a mass murderer."

"Dr. Maxene." Lavelle looked around carefully. "I'm going to tell you something that might hook up with how Mae West died. But you gotta promise not to tell anyone you got it from me."

St. Clair signaled for the cabby to wait. He slapped down the meter and pointed at it.

Lavelle leaned close. "The night Mae died, she may have seen somebody else."

"Some other man pick her up?"

"No. I just seen one dude pick her up that night. I'm talking about after that."

"She saw someone else?"

"She might have. I can't say for sure. But if she did, that could be why she died."

"Lavelle, stop being so mysterious. Who is this person?"

"I don't know the name, but I recognized one of those pictures you was showing around tonight. It was the picture with everybody in it."

"Somebody who was in that photo with Mae West and the man she was sitting on?"

"Go to North Avenue at Twenty-first Street," Lavelle said, getting into the cab. "Maybe you'll find out."

"Wait, Lavelle. North Avenue at Twenty-first is where the cab picked up Mae West. I've been there. There's nothing but houses and stores."

"Keep going. One night, somebody will be there."

"Why?"

"I don't know the name."

The cab driver shifted into gear, then gunned out of the turnaround. A hand gripped her arm. St. Clair half shrieked.

"Take it easy, Max." Grabowski's grip tightened. "You shouldn't be standing outside alone. I could have been anybody."

CHAPTER

16

THE MOON HAD laid a silver path across Lake Michigan from the horizon to Grabowski's porch. A freighter crossed the silver band, black as a shadow, and disappeared again into the darkness. The water was so still that the beam of silver light seemed like a solid walkway leading around the curve of the earth.

"For this I put up with a wall of ice across the street in winter," Grabowski said. He sank into a porch chair with a sigh and rummaged in the cooler. A few chunks of ice clinked among the water and cans of beer.

St. Clair sat on the porch steps and kicked off her shoes. She stretched out her legs, letting the silver path connect her to the shining orb across the lake. A breeze ruffled her hair. She brushed a mosquito off her arm.

"We're looking in the wrong direction, Grabowski."

"You think Simonson isn't our man, but he's the only one we know who ever made contact with Nanette Myer in the inner city, which is where she was when she got the poison. He could have handed her the poison in any form—a piece of candy, even. It's too easy to poison people; I'm surprised more husbands don't keel over."

"What if Aaron did see Nanette there? That doesn't mean he killed her. With the evidence you have so far, there's no way to prove your hypothesis."

"This is a murder investigation, Max, not a research lab."

"Not so different. In research, the task is to find the answer to a hypothesis that you think up. The answer you

129

find depends on your question. Ask the wrong question, get the wrong answer."

"I have to admit we're not getting anywhere with the questions we're asking."

"We should have more answers by now—at least know a few reasons why someone would want her dead."

"What about the husband? She was fooling around to the point that Myer put a detective on her. That might push some husbands over the edge."

"I don't honestly think he cared that much. He just wanted to know what she was doing."

"What about his reputation?"

St. Clair shook her head. "His reputation was secure as long as Nanette kept her strange activities quiet. Only a few people within medical circles knew about it. Doctors are used to keeping secrets—their patients' secrets, each other's medical blunders, social indiscretions."

"Then let's go back to Simonson," Grabowski said. "He had some sort of post-marital relationship with her; you admit that yourself. In that photo she was fawning all over him, but he was looking like he wished she would go away. Maybe he wanted to call it off, and she wouldn't."

"My previous reasoning holds," Maxene retorted. "Why should he care? Medical reputations are not ruined by social behaviors."

"But it was foolproof. He was out on North Avenue where no one could trace him. Or her."

"Lots of people knew about her. Rolondo, Lavelle, the nurses at the health clinic. With just a little information, we picked up her trail and his. They were both being too obvious, and poison is a devious method of murder. It doesn't fit. It had to be someone else."

"I don't agree. You say Simonson is the kind of person who likes to have people do what he says. If he still felt strongly about his ex-wife—whether he loved her or hated her—he would have gone out to North Avenue to straighten her out. And if she tried to drag him into her new life on North Avenue, he might have murdered her, just to make sure she was doing what he wanted—getting out of there."

"No one would kill an ex-wife just because she refused to do what he wanted," Maxene said.

"You'd be surprised what people will do."

Maxene's voice rose. "But we still don't know what Nanette was doing out on North Avenue, or who else she could have met there. Lavelle told me this very evening that Nanette might have met someone else on Twenty-first and North that night." St. Clair put a hand over her mouth, realizing Lavelle told her not to tell. Fortunately, Grabowski hadn't been listening.

"I admit we still have too many gaps in her days and nights," he said. "Lots of people knew where she was, but nobody knows what she was doing. Her husband and former husband both knew where she was, the pimps and prostitutes knew her by sight, even the doctor at the public health clinic treated her. Luigi talked to her. I'll bet we turn up a dozen public-health nurses who've watched her walk down the street. The detective her husband sent spotted her right away. She was either incredibly stupid or she wanted to be seen."

"Then we should be able to find someone who knew what she was doing. Maybe we'll even find some kind of evidence that points us to the murderer."

"That's too easy. But I think you're right. She was killed by someone who spotted her as easily as all the others did, but who managed to stay hidden. I wonder if Nanette even knew the person who killed her, which may be why we never find the murderer. It won't be the only unsolved crime in Milwaukee. My files are full of them."

St. Clair thought that over and couldn't come to any conclusion. She backtracked. "What else did Aaron Simonson say about what happened the night Nanette died?"

"Just that he picked her up and drove her home."

"But she went back to North Avenue," St. Clair persisted.

Grabowski sighed. "Or your friend Simonson never did drive her home." He held up a hand at St. Clair's protest.

"Okay, assuming that he did, why didn't she stay home? Why did she go back to North Avenue?"

St. Clair had a ready answer. "Hank was out of town that night. What was she going to do, watch television? She wasn't that kind of person. She liked to party."

"Why not call up a nice friend and party in a safe place? Or go to a movie."

Maxene scowled. "You still think Simonson didn't drive her home. You think he poisoned her and drove away."

"Look at the evidence, Max. Nanette was found by the taxi driver, dressed in prostitute garb, on North Avenue near her car. Not at home."

"She could have caught a cab back to the inner city."

"No cabs reported picking up a white woman dressed as a prostitute from a fancy east side address and taking her to Twenty-first and North. The only cab who reported taking her anywhere that night picked her up on North Avenue when she looked ill and dropped her off at the ER."

"She could have taken a bus from her home up North Avenue."

"No bus drivers remember picking her up. We passed her photo around. Only a few buses run at that hour, and she would have been the only white face on the North Avenue run. No, Max. It boils down to this: Lavelle was with Mrs. Myer about ten when Aaron Simonson picked her up. Simonson also performed the autopsy and produced a finding of heart failure."

"But he saved blood and tissue for a possible later investigation."

"He saved it for all violent deaths. If he hadn't, that would have been noticed."

"Okay, if Simonson did poison her, where did Simonson get the poison?"

"Out of your unlocked, unguarded lunchroom refrigerator at Marquette."

"But it was six months ago when I closed my research!"

"This is a methodical man who saves blood and tissue for all cases of violent death, just in case a policeman asks for them. This is a man who locks himself in a lab for days at a time, just to catch up with work. He's similar to Dr. Gaust and Nathan Schalz. I've read their research reports. They all plan their lives months—hell, years—in advance. Plus, we have a witness who saw Simonson pick up Nanette that night—Lavelle."

Maxene sighed. "You've lost your witness. Lavelle went to Alabama."

"What!" Grabowski grabbed her arm. St. Clair yelped with pain.

"Sorry." Grabowski took hold of the other arm. "What did you say about Alabama?"

"She's on her way. She and Rolondo came into the ER tonight. She got beat up again and split open her stitches. Rolondo said he'd either pay for a plastic surgeon and keep her working for him, or she'd have to take a cheap sew job from me and could leave for Alabama. She opted for Alabama, and told me she was getting a ride to Chicago with a friend. She didn't want Rolondo changing his mind."

Grabowski sat back in his chair. The moonlight lighted and shadowed his face at the same time.

"Doesn't it seem coincidental to you that our only witness for that evening is on her way to Alabama, transportation unknown? Simonson is getting his key witness out of the way."

"How could a pathologist meddle in Rolondo's business relationships?"

"Rolondo is easy to find. Why do you keep standing up for Simonson?"

St. Clair lifted her hands. "Blind faith."

Grabowski laughed. His face, caught in the light of the moon, was flat planes of white and black, with shadows for eyes. He leaned toward her and slid a hand behind her neck. His lips were cool and tasted of beer.

Inside the house, the phone rang.

"Hell!" Grabowski snapped. He slammed into the house. St. Clair could hear him snarling into the phone. The screen door slammed again, and he stood over her in the shadows.

"I have to go downtown. Something came up in another case. I don't want to leave you here alone, so I've called a patrol car to cruise by here from time to time, and I can call Lemie to stay, if you want."

"Don't be silly. I'll be fine."

"I worry about you. Everybody at that hospital knows where you are. Either I call Lemie or you go inside and lock the door. Open it only for me." This time his kiss was a perfunctory tap on the cheek.

St. Clair sat on the porch a few more minutes, after the taillights of his car disappeared around the corner. The moonlight wasn't silvery now. A breeze had sprung up, rippling the water. The path to the horizon was treacherous. She kept thinking over the people who knew Nanette Myer, people who might have known why she went to North Avenue, people she might have confided in, people who might guess what she did during that blank hour and a half.

When her thoughts got to Virginia, she stopped thinking about Nanette and started thinking about Virginia. Grabowski was right. Virginia had always planned her life years in advance. She knew exactly what experiments she would be doing on a certain day. That was why her research was so easily funded. Her proposals read like battle plans. But, if Nathan were right, Virginia had recently started spending money on nonbudgeted items. If St. Clair hadn't seen the evidence with her own eyes, she wouldn't have believed it. St. Clair had agreed to break into Virginia's office with Nathan because Nathan had convinced her Virginia needed help. So far, St. Clair had done nothing to help. She went inside to dial Virginia's home number. No answer. She tried the lab. Nathan answered.

"Virginia left about eight," he said. "She went out to dinner." He hesitated.

"With Hank Myer?"

"Yes. Can I tell her to call you?"

"Don't bother." She hung up. Remnants of jealous curiosity made her want to dial Hank Myer's number, but she fought the temptation. Now she was totally awake and it was only 1:00 in the morning. The week before, she had planned to play tennis at this hour. She paced the kitchen, her bare feet gritting on the sandy linoleum. She stared at the beer in the refrigerator. Finally, she grabbed her purse and car keys and stalked out through the moonlight to her car. Nathan was awake and working. She had spent many night hours talking through her research with Nathan. He listened well, and she needed to talk.

Nathan was hard at work behind a new complicated-looking machine that bubbled and hissed. Red buttons flashed, timers ticked, liquid churned. He jumped when she opened the door.

"Max! What are you doing here? And what happened? Were you in a car accident?"

"It's a long story, Nathan, all about Nanette Myer. Some-body thinks I know more than I do about how she died." St. Clair sat on an overturned crate marked LABORATORY MICE: 100. The odor still clung.

"And you drove here alone in the middle of the night? Are you crazy?"

"I needed to talk, and I knew you were a captive audi-ence. The big gap in Nanette Myer's death is where she went for the hour and a half before she died. We know Dr. Simonson picked her up about ten, and we know she was back on North Avenue at eleven-forty. But how did she get back to North Avenue? The police are combing the city for taxi drivers, bus drivers, anybody who might have seen her get picked up or dropped off that night."

Nathan was staring at her, his eyes wide. "Sunday night? Max! Are you telling me she died Sunday night?"

"When did you think?"

"The funeral was days after that. I never even wondered what day she died."

"So why is it important?"

"She called here Sunday night. I was working late, and she called because her car ran out of gas, and she needed a ride."

"I didn't know she even knew you," St. Clair said, surprised.

Nathan flushed. "We met at some party at Virginia's. After that, she came down here a couple of times in the evening after her class, when I was working late. She said there was no one home, and she was lonely. We used to talk. She would explore around the lab and ask about the equipment and the experiments. She was nice, Maxene, although she sure hated doctors. She said they treated people like victims."

"So when she called you Sunday night, you dropped everything to go pick her up."

He nodded. "She said Dr. Myer was out of town and all her friends were asleep."

"Where was she?"

"That was the odd thing. She was at her house. I don't know why she couldn't have waited until morning to get her car, but she said she had an early class, and she needed her car right then. So I drove her back to her car. It was somewhere off North Avenue. Terrible part of town. She's lucky that whoever picked her up didn't mug her."

"Was her car actually out of gas?"

"I assumed so. We had brought the gas can for her lawnmower, and I poured some gas into her tank. She drove off."

St. Clair frowned, trying to fit this in. One more piece of the puzzle had fallen into place. This meant Aaron Simonson was telling the truth. He had brought Nanette home. He hadn't been the last person to see her before she died.

Nathan had.

St. Clair stood up from the mouse crate. Things were getting confusing again. Would Nathan have killed Nanette? That meant that Nathan tried to strangle St. Clair in her apartment; Nathan had set the ball machine on her. Nathan knew she was going to be at the tennis club that night. St. Clair started out the door.

"Wait, Max. Where are you going?"

"Home. Or what passes for it these days."

"But we didn't finish going through Virginia's desk. We were interrupted the other night."

"Nathan, don't involve me in your little feud with Virginia. I already know she's lying to her granting foundation. I already know her research is going nowhere, and she's pretending that it is."

"What if there's something you could do to help her out? If you looked through her things again, maybe you would know what to do."

St. Clair raised a skeptical eyebrow. What she really wanted was to get out of there and think over what she had just learned. Breaking into another professor's office with a possible murderer was idiotic, even insane. This could be an easy opportunity for Nathan to throttle her. Her fingers went to her throat.

"I told the police I was here," she said lamely.

Nathan looked at her blankly. "Are you planning to tell them you're going to commit burglary?"

Not the remark of a murderer, St. Clair decided, wildly. She followed Nathan down the hall to Virginia's office.

This time it took only half an hour to find what she wanted. St. Clair rose from her cramped position on the floor behind Virginia's desk and stretched her neck. Her back seemed to be bent permanently. Nathan yawned and stuffed the notebook he was reading back into the drawer.

"Nothing," he said. "Not a decimal out of place. Her statistics are consistent all the way through; her drug quantities are constant, her conclusions fit the data they're based on, and she isn't any closer to a pharmacological breakthrough than I am."

The sky was clear, and the stars bright enough to penetrate the city lights and ozone. St. Clair sat in her car thinking about what she had not told Nathan. In her purse was Virginia's proposal to a European drug company introducing her new bacteriocidal leprosy drug, proposing they start testing it on humans. It was a risky proposal for a drug that didn't even show high marks on mice. European regulations for human testing were slight compared to American standards, but even a European board of health would raise their eyebrows at the data this proposal was based on.

If they saw the data. The proposal referred to positive results, promised conclusively that the drug would work. Virginia couldn't make these assertions and also give the drug company the data St. Clair had seen. Had she made up data and presented fictitious results?

It had been done before, and by the most disciplined of researchers whose ethics cracked after years of failed experiments, decades of crushed hope. Virginia was forty-five. She may have fallen into the trap of believing in her drug beyond what her experiments proved. She may be so desperate that she was willing to risk disaster rather than continue years of inconclusive research.

The ice that Virginia was going out on was too thin. If the drug were approved for testing on humans in Europe, based on Virginia's promises of positive results, and the testing proved ineffective, Virginia's credibility was gone forever. Her career was toast.

St. Clair's first urge was to drive immediately to Virginia's house and confront her. She resisted. Initial urges were risky, medically and socially. Besides, Virginia wasn't home. Tomorrow was soon enough.

In the meantime, she was wide awake and free of the confining police presence of Grabowski. Go to Twenty-first and North Avenue, Lavelle had said. Maybe it was different at night. A detour down North Avenue couldn't be that dangerous. She wouldn't even get out of her car.

At 2:00 A.M. in Milwaukee, even North Avenue was quiet. The elms on Twenty-first Street that shaded it during the hot days turned it into a black tunnel at night. St. Clair parked by the side door of the grocery and turned off her engine and lights. A man and woman were strolling up the sidewalk, arms around each other. They seemed harmless. St. Clair got out of the car. What was so special about this intersection?

Two women were coming toward her, the rhinestones on their jeans flashing in the faint streetlights off North Avenue. Their high heels clicked on the sidewalk. St. Clair stepped forward.

"I wonder if you can help me," she said, trying to sound casual. "I'm looking for a place Lavelle Taylor told me about."

The women stopped but didn't answer.

"Lavelle told me to come to Twenty-first and North. She said it's where she came."

The women looked at each other.

"Lavelle ain't here," one said.

"I know. She went to Alabama. When she left, she told me to come here, but she didn't say which house."

The woman shrugged, a faint jingle of jewelry in the dark. A wave of perfume drifted on the hot night breeze. "I wouldn't advise it, honey, but if that's what you want, it's upstairs." She jerked her head toward the grocery.

St. Clair crossed the dark sidewalk and tried the door. Unlocked, but unoccupied. Not a glimmer of light came down the stairs. The women were watching her.

"Not there now?" the woman asked. "Can you wait till next week?"

"I really don't want to."

"There's a number you can call if you can't wait too long. I don't have it, but I know somebody who does. Call me tomorrow. After noon." She rattled off her phone number.

St. Clair hurried to her car to write it down.

Balmy night air does nothing to wake up a sleepy person. St. Clair's eyelids were barely open when she pulled into Grabowski's weedy driveway. Grabowski's car was parked in the garage. She turned her lights off so as not to waken him. She coasted to a stop and eased the door closed. Her bare feet gritted on the sandy kitchen floor.

The kitchen light went on, half blinding her. In the glare of the single bulb, the dull linoleum floor, crumb-spattered, vinyl-topped table, and coffee-stained sink stood out in horrible clarity. The bare bulb swung in the breeze.

Grabowski was standing by the light switch, rumpled, unshaven, wearing flowered Aloha shorts. He was also holding a gun, pointed straight at St. Clair.

"It's me," she whispered, feeling like a rabbit caught in headlights. She could hardly breathe. What if his hand were unsteady from being wakened, and he accidently pulled the trigger? Plenty of family members were mistaken for burglars. St. Clair had treated the survivors in the ER.

Grabowski lowered the gun slowly. His jaw clenched. He placed the gun on the counter and turned off the light. His footsteps crunched on the gritty floor, then the couch squeaked. St. Clair crept toward the bedroom and crawled to the center of the big, safe bed.

When she woke the next morning, Grabowski was gone. A note under the coffee pot said he would call at 11:00 and if there was no answer, he would put out an APB and have her arrested. The note was scribbled on the back of his law school acceptance letter. The grease-speckled stove clock read 10:45. She poured herself a cup of cold coffee, added cream, sugar, and a handful of ice cubes.

Not too early to phone a prostitute, she decided. She dialed the number, hoping she was reading her scrawl correctly. No answer. She picked a couple of sweet rolls from Grabowski's seemingly inexhaustible supply and carried them out to the porch. She watched the sailboats on Lake Michigan and thought over what she had learned the night before.

First, Nathan had admitted he brought Nanette back to North Avenue, which let Aaron off the hook but put Nathan on.

Second, Virginia probably had not lost her grant money. She was just spending it on something other than what she had stated in her grant. This was not unusual. Researchers often got deep into their research and found they needed equipment or supplies different from those anticipated. The correct way to handle this was to write an amendment to the grant, submit that, and have it approved. There was usually no problem in approval, but the process took weeks.

Valuable time would be lost, especially if the grant were for a specified period, like one academic year, and not for a specific amount of money. Many recipients simply purchased what they needed, even if it wasn't approved on the grant. They hoped the granting foundation would never find out, or that positive research results would balance out the deception if it did. Most of the time the grantors never found out. If they did, however, they had the right to yank the grant and never issue another. It happened often enough to make everyone wary.

Third, Virginia had written a new drug proposal based on results not found on any data sheet. Last night, St. Clair had concluded that Virginia was inventing data without sending her funding source any proof. But any drug company would eventually demand proof, St. Clair reminded herself. Virginia must have fictitious data sheets stored somewhere in the university computer or at home. Most likely at home.

The more St. Clair thought about it, the more she became convinced that talking to Virginia was her next step. It was her duty as a friend to help Virginia get herself out of a tight spot. And it was her duty as a member of the university community to prevent research fraud. One researcher would ruin the reputation of an entire university. Everyone's grants might dry up.

She went inside and dialed Virginia's office. The phone rang ten times before Nathan answered.

"She taught her nine o'clock class, then went to her office for about an hour," he reported. "Then she told the secretary she was ill, and she went home."

"Does she know we were in her office last night?"

"She didn't say anything about it."

St. Clair hung up and started rooting around in her purse for her address book with Virginia's unlisted phone number. Before she found it, the phone rang. It was Grabowski. She put a Danish into the toaster oven.

"Where did you go last night?" he demanded.

"I didn't know where you were, so I couldn't tell you. Are you upset?"

"Of course I'm upset. I have you at my house for your own safety. If you don't want to be safe, you can go home."

St. Clair decided not to answer. It was too easy to get into a verbal sparring match that led nowhere. Grabowski broke the silence.

"Where were you?"

"I went to the university to talk to Nathan."

"You walked through that mugger's heaven into that stinking pit alone in the middle of the night?"

"If you're referring to the pharmacology lab, yes. There's no need to shout."

"Maxene, that place is a setup for a mugging. Even if there weren't somebody out there gunning for you, it's stupid for a lone woman to go there. And you've got only one good arm. Do you think just because you're a doctor, you're immune?"

"Immune?"

"Yes, immune. From getting seriously injured."

"Immune."

"Maxene, what's that crackling noise? It sounds like a fire."

St. Clair threw a handful of salt at the flames licking out of the toaster oven. She flipped her blackened sweet roll onto the counter and shook her smarting fingers. "You could use a cleaning lady in here once a week, Grabowski. Sugar and crumbs ignite when they pile up in the bottom of a toaster."

"Let's get back on topic, Maxene. Why did you go to Marquette last night, and what were you thinking a minute ago? When you get that distracted tone in your voice, I know you're ready to take off for parts unknown."

"I was thinking about what you just said about doctors feeling immune. That's part of what this case revolves around—doctors feeling immune. Everywhere there are doctors taking matters into their own hands and doing things any other human would know was wrong. Aaron Simonson knew Nanette was pretending to be a prostitute in the inner city, and he did nothing until it was too late. Hank did the same thing, and then he wanted to ignore his wife's blood results. The surgery resident at St. Agnes' ordered up a meal for a dead person so he could eat free."

"And you follow leads alone in the inner city when even a police detective would call for help."

"I'm as guilty as the others. The right or wrong of what doctors do blurs. We've been trained to assess a situation to the limits of our ability, then do what we think is right. If results backfire, we try something else. But taking immediate action based on our personal assessments—and accepting the medical consequences—is what we're trained to do. What we aren't trained to do is accept the personal consequences. We act as if we ourselves are immune to any consequences—physical, emotional, psychological."

"Doctors have always considered themselves immune, Max. History is full of doctors who made house calls during smallpox epidemics. Or doctors who experimented on themselves with vaccines. Brave people."

"They just believed so fervently in their therapy and their own invincibility that they had no hesitation giving themselves the drug. The attitude shows a certain contempt for societal rules. Doctors who believe they're immune from consequences can believe they're immune from societal boundaries."

"What are you telling me, Max? That a doctor committed this murder? I've been saying that all along."

"But not Hank. Or Aaron Simonson."

"Try to put aside how fond you are of these men, Maxene." His voice was cool.

"I'm not saying it was a doctor. It could be someone with the doctor mentality, someone who believes he or she is above the law because of a personal mission."

"All criminals think they're above the law. But, okay, we'll look for someone with a deity complex. Tell me when you come up with a name and a face. Character sketches and motivation theories fit lots of people. Now tell me what you found out last night and make it quick. I have a string of people waiting to see me."

She gave him a quick review of what Nathan had told her. "So now we know Aaron didn't kill Nanette. Nathan saw her after Aaron took her home."

"Why didn't he tell me this when I talked to him before?"

"You didn't ask the right question."

He sighed. "No more detecting, Max. Stay right there until you leave for St. Agnes. I'll stop by the ER at midnight and follow you home. Don't leave without me, understand?"

St. Clair rolled her eyes and hung up. She warmed another sweet roll, watching out for fires, then showered and dressed. She still wanted to talk to Virginia. A slight detour on her way to St. Agnes' wouldn't matter. She phoned Virginia and told her she wanted to stop by her house at noon.

Virginia Gaust lived only a few blocks from St. Clair's apartment, but the neighborhood was vastly different. Her brick cottage sat on a corner lot, the stone wall dotted with pots of geraniums. The flower garden looked like it was copied from a gardening magazine. Virginia had come out of her divorce a lot better than Maxene had.

A chime tinkled as St. Clair pushed open the front gate. She stood on the flagstone walk looking up at the gabled roof that hung, thatchlike, over curved leaded windows. No one answered the door, even after several rings.

She banged the heavy brass knocker a few times, then walked around the house, stepping on the carefully laid stone steps that outlined the herb garden. Dark green sprigs of rosemary mingled with parsley and varieties of oregano. Dwarf red and yellow dahlias brightened the green backdrop of the ivy-covered wall. She rounded the corner of the house, drawn by the musky scent of roses. A clematis trailed over the brick garage, purple blossoms dripping with water. St. Clair moved closer to sniff their fragrance. It was muted with the smells of the garage—oil, gasoline, and something else. Exhaust.

She wrenched at the doorknob of the side door. A wave of exhaust hit her in the face. Inside, Virginia's car was purring quietly.

"Virginia!" she shouted. She fumbled in her purse for her handkerchief and plunged into the dark building, handkerchief over her mouth. Her eyes watered, and she felt sick to her stomach. She pulled open the car door and switched off the ignition. No one was in the car.

The car's overhead light didn't work, and the light from the open garage door wasn't strong enough to pierce the shadows filling the floor of the backseat. The smell of exhaust was choking her. She backed out of the car and tried to open the back door of the car. Locked. She reached through the front door to unlock it, still holding the handkerchief over her mouth. Behind her, a shadow moved.

She turned to see who it was. Silhouetted in the light from the door was an upraised arm. Holding a wrench. The wrench dropped.

St. Clair threw up an arm. The damaged arm. The blow hit like fire ripping through her. Her scream echoed through the damp brick of the garage. She screamed again and again, sobbing, trying to shield her arm. She crawled into the car to get away from her shadowy attacker and huddled on the floor of the front seat.

"Stop!" she screamed. "What are you doing!" But the blows rained on, smashing the glass of the window, denting the metal. She unlocked the passenger side and slid onto the garage floor, wriggling under the car. The blows stopped.

It was too dark under the car to see where the person was standing. She could feel blood running down her hand on the inside of the bandage. Her head throbbed, and nausea flooded her. The smell of exhaust was less now. The side door to the garage had been open, and the car had been turned off. At least she wouldn't be poisoned by fumes, she thought.

"Help!" she began screaming. This was a populated neighborhood. Rich people had brick garden walls around their houses, but they still had ears. Surely someone would call the police. If Virginia's car were here, Virginia had to be here, too. Maybe she had been in the shower when St. Clair was ringing the doorbell. Maybe she had been working in her study in the basement. Virginia would call the police.

There was no sound around her in the garage. The person had left. She rolled out from under the car and got to her knees. Then something struck the back of her head, and she dropped to the floor.

CHAPTER

17

DETECTIVE JOSEPH GRABOWSKI was tired of letting his emotions play around with him. He sat dejected at his desk, eating a salami sandwich and staring at the pile of documents that slithered across the nicked oak desktop. Pathology reports, telephone company reports, eyewitness accounts, notes from his own notebook. He'd gone over them and over them until he know everything by memory. Facts should be falling into order by now, and they weren't. The dead woman's motivation for hanging around the dirtiest, noisiest, and most morally corrupting district of Milwaukee was still a mystery. Curiosity wasn't enough, as Maxene had pointed out. What had kept Nanette Myer going there?

Dr. Simonson's part in the dead woman's actions was also a mystery, as was Dr. Myer's decision to let his wife continue roaming around North Avenue after he knew what she was doing. To make everything more difficult, Grabowski's only sources of objective information were a prostitute who had vanished and a pimp who viewed truth as a variable commodity. Grabowski wished he were back investigating rapes. At least the motives were clear.

Grabowski sighed, thinking of all the doctors involved in this case. He was sick of doctors. Every time he talked to one he felt like a meter was running. Doctors looked at their watches every thirty seconds, or checked their beepers to make sure they were still working. They carried themselves with a preoccupied air as if they were involved in something more important than the person who was talking. They reminded Grabowski of lawyers.

None of the doctors he had met so far left him feeling like they were telling the truth. Including Maxene. But, as Maxene had pointed out, doctors' work involved keeping other people's secrets. Keeping their own secrets from the police would be child's play. Maxene also said that doctors considered themselves immune from just about anything, since they themselves had witnessed nearly every sort of accident or illness and emerged untouched. Maxene also talked about victims, a topic where Grabowski was an expert. However, he couldn't figure out how victims fit into this scene any differently than they did in any other crime.

All right, he decided, pulling a clean sheet of paper toward him. Who exactly is keeping secrets? Dr. Simonson? Dr. Myer? Dr. Gaust? Dr. St. Clair? He flung down the pencil in disgust. A physical wave of emotion washed through him. Anger, frustration, jealousy. Why had Maxene slept with Hank Myer the very night his wife died? Did doctors just leap into bed with each other at the drop of a hat? Maxene's ex-husband had, and Maxene seemed to think they all did. Once she said the hospital on-call rooms were virtual motels. Grabowski had thought she was making a joke. Maybe it was the bald truth.

Something about Dr. Myer bothered Grabowski more than other doctors bothered him, and it wasn't just his attachment to Maxene. Grabowski was old enough to accept a woman's attachment to another man. No, he was bothered by the secrets that Myer must be keeping. Simonson was keeping secrets, too. Grabowski could feel it. He glanced at his watch. Twelve-thirty. Time to find out.

First, a detour up North Avenue.

Grabowski found Rolondo the pimp in an air-conditioned apartment over the abandoned storefront across from Luigi's Deli. He was lounging in a leather recliner playing poker with two other men. Hundred dollar bills were scattered over the table. The whine of the window air conditioner was drowned by the blast of music from a sound system that could have handled a concert in Washington Park.

Grabowski slammed the door to make his presence known.

Rolondo looked up from his card game and snapped his fingers at a girl who had come out of the kitchen. She turned down the noise slightly and disappeared, closely followed by the two poker players.

Grabowski dropped into a chair.

"I ain't done nothing," Rolondo said.

"Quit whining," Grabowski snapped. "I know exactly what you've done, and it's enough for me to drag you in any time I want."

"Then why don't you?"

"Because I don't care what you've done. I care what someone else has done."

A slight smile twitched Rolondo's lips. Grabowski shook his head. "No bargains, pimp. Tell me or go to jail."

"Tell you what?" Rolondo lit a long brown cigarette and pouted around it.

"I want the name of the person who had sex with Lavelle Taylor while Mae West watched."

"Don't know, man. I wasn't there, and the dude didn't pay by check." He chuckled.

"Find Lavelle."

"Gone."

Grabowski glared at him. "Then find me somebody who looks just like her. I want her waiting for me in the place where Lavelle took Mae West and the man."

"It's downstairs, man. No problem about that."

"Have her there in half an hour." He slammed the door again on the way out.

Grabowski got into his hot squad car longing for a beer. Was he becoming an alcoholic? The thought nagged him occasionally, like when he saw the plastic sacks full of empty beer cans lining his garage, waiting to be recycled. Maxene hadn't said anything about them. Maybe she hadn't noticed. Maxene. He gunned the engine and squealed off the sidewalk.

Dr. Simonson was not in the lab at St. Agnes. The doors were locked, and no one answered Grabowski's pounding. Neither was he in the cafeteria or at home when Grabowski

called from the reception desk at the ER. Next, he called
Dr. Myer's office.

Dr. Myer wasn't at his office either, but he was expected
back shortly. "Call him on his car phone and tell him I'm
coming," Grabowski told the receptionist who answered the
phone. He went out to his car and radioed in a request to
locate Simonson's car. If it were parked in Milwaukee, a
patrol car would spot it soon. Doctors insisted upon driving
new, flashy cars.

Dr. Myer's receptionist didn't want to let Grabowski in.
Neither did she want to let him wait in the empty waiting room. Grabowski ignored her and pushed through the
swinging door into the clinic and found his own way to
Dr. Myer's frigid oriental hideout. Myer was just hanging
up the phone. He scowled at Grabowski.

"Push me too hard, and I call my attorney," he snapped.

"So call," Grabowski said. He took his time deciding
which leather chair to sit in.

Myer glared at him. "When are you going to let Dr. St.
Clair live in her own apartment?" The papers under his
agitated elbow fluttered to the floor.

Grabowski crossed his legs and grinned. "Maxene's a big
girl. She can go home any time she wants. But I'm not here
to talk about where you or I think Maxene should be living.
I'm here to talk about your wife."

"I've told you everything." Myer glanced at his watch.

"I have a feeling we'll be interrupted if we stay here
to chat," Grabowski said pleasantly. "You have an empty
waiting room. Why don't we go for a drive?"

"Where to?" Myer's eyes narrowed. His hand crept toward
the phone.

"I'm not arresting you; I'm offering you a free tour of
Milwaukee. Why are people so suspicious of police?" He
held open the door.

Grabowski's unmarked squad car had collected some
eggs and rotten vegetables earlier, when he had parked
it near Rolondo's. Myer looked at the yellow and green
smears and grimaced.

"Shall we take my car?" he offered. He jerked his head toward a white Mercedes.

"I need my radio."

Grabowski drove south on Oakland and turned west on North Avenue. The traffic got slower and louder. He looked over at Myer, who didn't seem to be watching where they were going. Finally they pulled up in front of the storefront where Rolondo's prostitute would be waiting. Grabowski turned off the motor and radioed in his location. Myer looked around.

"If this is your idea of a nice place to chat, I'd hate to see where you take Maxene for dinner," he said.

"Get out."

A blanket covered the cracked window of the storefront. The heat was intense, magnified by the crushing odor of decaying garbage and dry rot. A mattress covered by an India print bedspread was on the floor. Grabowski had seen worse, but not by much. He let Myer step ahead of him and look around. There was no one in the room.

"You have friends who live here?" Myer said.

Grabowski smiled. He was going to enjoy this. "No, but somebody related to you used to spend her time here. She even had your last name."

Myer swung around and lashed out with a clenched fist. The blow caught Grabowski on the jaw, knocking his head backward. He bounced off the wall and came back, head low, hands high. He gave Myer a jab to the stomach, another jab to the side of the head. Myer flopped on the mattress, groaning and retching. A trickle of blood ran down his lip.

Grabowski flexed his fingers and debated whether to hit him again, just to make himself feel better. He decided not. Myer staggered to his feet.

"I can get you pulled off the police force for this," Myer gasped.

"Your word against mine, Doc."

Myer groaned and sank down on the mattress again. "You want me to say I knew Nanette was out here acting like a prostitute, having sex with whoever would pay? I'm not going to say that. She was here, but she wasn't into sex. She just hung around and watched."

"That's right, Doc. She wasn't into sex. She was into watching. You were the one into sex, and she watched. Right here on this mattress. Making it with a black woman named Lavelle."

"You can't prove it."

"Yes, I can." Grabowski banged on the wall.

The door behind the mattress clicked open, and a black woman stepped out, hair in corn rows, with purple eye shadow, scarlet lipstick. Not Lavelle, but close enough to fool Myer, Grabowski hoped. Myer had only seen her briefly.

Myer got slowly to his feet. "What the hell," he sighed. "I don't know if that's the girl or not. But I didn't kill my wife, even if I wanted to, seeing her standing there in that awful wig and that skirt, grinning like she was insane."

"Why did you pick up Lavelle and tell your wife to watch?"

"To shock her. To make her realize what a horrible place this was. To get her to cut out her weird act and come home. It didn't work."

The radio was crackling when they got back to the squad car. Grabowski called in. His lips tightened, and he slammed down the receiver. He gunned the car in a crazy U-turn.

"Maxene and Virginia Gaust were found unconscious in Dr. Gaust's garage. They've been taken to St. Agnes ER," he said.

Hank Myer had wiped the blood from his face by the time Grabowski swung up to Myer's clinic. Myer opened the door, then stopped.

"You have no reason to do me any favors," he said, not looking at Grabowski, "but I'm going to ask you anyway. Don't tell Maxene about me and my wife and that awful storefront, will you? People do strange things when they're angry. I don't want Maxene to know."

Grabowski let a minute go by before he answered. "I don't know how the subject would come up," he said.

CHAPTER

18

VIRGINIA HAD NOT called the police. The simple reason was that Virginia was found on the garage floor behind the car, dizzy and sick from being hit over the head with the same wrench that hit Maxene.

Neighbors had called the police. The ambulance took them both to St. Agnes Hospital, at Maxene's mumbled request. Virginia went first to the emergency room, where her bloodwork showed she had inhaled little of the exhaust fumes. St. Clair had interrupted her attacker soon after the motor was turned on. Virginia's head wound was not serious, but she elected to stay the night.

St. Clair went to surgery. Again.

Grabowski told all this to Maxene about two hours later, after she got out of surgery. The bone in her arm wasn't broken, but the amount of blood lost from where the stitches had been torn from the previous wound made the surgeon decide to repair it in surgery rather than in the ER.

"Don't do this anymore, Max," Grabowski said. His face was pale and his lips tight. "You should have called me when you went to Dr. Gaust's house. You're lucky the squad car got there when it did."

"I needed to talk to Virginia about her research," St. Clair mumbled. "She wouldn't have talked if a cop had been sitting there."

"You're being followed by a homicidal maniac," Grabowski said. "This isn't the time to drop in on friends for a quiet chat."

Maxene St. Clair began to cry. Grabowski had seen a lot of people cry. They cried under pressure, when they were cornered, when they were injured, when they were frightened. He had learned how to wait out the tears and let the person get under control. These tears were from exhaustion, he knew, but it didn't make him feel any better. He took her hand and waited until she was drying her eyes on the bedsheet.

"I'm sorry," she quavered. "It was stupid for me to go off alone."

He kissed her, relieved to see her dry-eyed. It was her resilience that had attracted him to her. He had watched her in the ER handle one disaster after another with calm good humor. Even at the end of ten hours she was tired but never down.

"I'm leaving you under the nurse's eye. Promise me you'll stay here until you're discharged and I take you home."

Out in the hall he met Dr. Myer coming out of the elevator.

"How is Maxene?" he demanded nervously. "The surgeon said she wasn't seriously injured. What happened?"

"From what Dr. Gaust says, first someone hit Dr. Gaust on the head when she was closing the door to her garage. The blow knocked her unconscious. Then the person turned on the car engine and closed up the garage. Dr. St. Clair found the car running and turned it off. Then she herself was attacked. She got inside the car and managed to avoid the worst of it."

"Dr. Myer," Grabowski continued, interrupting Myer's next question. "Where were you just before I got to your office at one o'clock. Your receptionist said you went to lunch at eleven forty-five? You were supposed to be back for a one o'clock appointment."

Myer looked confused. "Dr. Simonson called me, and we met for a bite to eat. He didn't have much time, so we picked up some sandwiches at the deli on North Oakland and we ate in Simonson's car."

"You sat in Dr. Simonson's car between twelve and twelve forty-five?"

"Part of that time we were picking up the sandwiches. Then I drove over to the Atwater Beach in Shorewood, and we parked in that parking lot that overlooks the beach. I left there before one, but it took about ten minutes to get back to the office. Traffic."

"Your office is less than a mile from Dr. Gaust's home."

"That's right."

"Did anyone see you at the beach?"

"Dr. Simonson, of course. It was a hot day, and there were lots of people parking there. No one I knew."

"Do you normally eat lunch in a park?"

"Usually we eat at St. Agnes cafeteria, since Aaron works there and I often make hospital rounds there after lunch."

"Why did you eat in his car this time?"

"I didn't have anybody in the hospital at St. Agnes and Dr. Simonson said he wanted to talk to me."

"What about?"

Myer clenched his jaw. "About my wife. Aaron thought I didn't know what Nanette had been doing on North Avenue, and also that I didn't know about his little affair with her. He thought I should hear it from him, before I got it from the police. Of course I've known all along. My wife used secrets as a power tool. She enjoyed telling people that she knew things about them—usually things they would have preferred no one else knew. She said that if doctors could know secrets, she could, too."

"So she created this bit of secret knowledge—that she was parading around North Avenue like a hooker—and she made sure you knew it," Grabowski said.

"She would drop funny little comments when we were out with friends and only, she and I knew what she was talking about. I couldn't shut her up."

"Someone shut her up."

"She probably knew something about the person and taunted them with it once too often," Myer concluded grimly.

The paging system blared out Myer's name. He looked at his watch. "I'm busy. You'll have to catch up with me later."

Instead, Grabowski followed Myer into the elevator. "Who else might have a secret that Nanette knew?"

"Everybody has secrets. Most people have phases of their lives they'd just as soon forget. That's why most doctors get divorced. The first wife knew them when they took orders from nurses and got yelled at by everybody on staff. Then they turn into big shots, and they want to forget they ever listened to a nurse. So they divorce the woman who remembers all that and who probably reminds them of it during angry moments. My wife was an expert at those reminders."

"Do you think your wife knew something about Aaron Simonson?"

"Why not? She was married to him, as you probably know. She married him when he was in medical school. Halfway through his residency, she figured out he would always be a pathologist on a lousy hospital salary. So she dumped him and went for the big money—me. For a while I deluded myself that they were just incompatible. But really, she was incompatible with an income under a hundred thousand. Being married for your money is not pleasant."

"Being divorced for lack of it could be worse. So why did he have a post-marital affair with her?"

"Nanette could twist him around her fingers. He would do anything she asked. She got lonely, and she called him up. She told him to come see her dressed up like a prostitute on North Avenue, and the idiot went."

"He took her home, where she didn't want to go."

"That's what he told me, too. The poor guy finally did the right thing instead of what she told him to do."

They paused at the entrance to the doctor's lounge. "Why don't you talk to Aaron yourself?" Myer said. His pager on his belt beeped. He glanced at the number on the top of the pager, then at his watch.

"We're talking to him now," Grabowski said. "Simonson's car was seen two blocks from Dr. Gaust's house just before noon. He had plenty of time to hit Dr. Gaust over the head, turn on the car, and beat up Dr. St. Clair with a wrench. We just arrested him for the murder of your wife and for the attempted murder of Dr. St. Clair and Dr. Gaust."

CHAPTER

19

ST. CLAIR SAT in her hospital room, frustrated and angry. The sun sank, and she still sat there alone, turning the events over and over in her mind. She didn't need to stay overnight in the hospital. She had pleaded with the surgeon, with the surgical resident, and with Grabowski. They had all patted her kindly on whatever part of her body was closest to them and told her that one night in the hospital wouldn't hurt. But now that she had time to think, she needed out. She had left messages for Grabowski everywhere she could think of, but he didn't call. She was on the verge of tears when Hank Myer walked into her room and astonished her by sitting on her bed and putting his arms around her.

"What's this all about?" she said into his collar. It seemed nice to rest her head there, so she did.

"I'm apologizing," he said. "When I saw you that day at the detective's house, I said some terrible things. Can you forgive me?"

"I already have. I was edgy myself. The police had been accusing me of the same thing. Your spending the night at my home the night of your wife's funeral didn't make either of us look good."

"The police know about that?"

"Milwaukee government may seem like an overburdened bureaucracy, but they do know how to keep tabs on their citizens. Even the street cleaners know who is having affairs."

Hank kissed her on the cheek, then sank into the visitor's chair. He looked exhausted.

157

"That idiot detective of yours arrested Aaron Simonson," he said. "I spent the last three hours arranging bail. It's bizarre to be doing that for the man who supposedly murdered my wife, but I know Aaron didn't do it. He couldn't have, any more than you could have. I keep apologizing to him for the blunder. I should keep apologizing to you."

"Grabowski arrested Aaron? He's making a big mistake!"

"Your stupid detective says Aaron's car was seen parked a few blocks from Virginia's house during the time you and Virginia were being attacked. Actually, the poor slob had parked in front of your house, which isn't that far from Virginia's. He was waiting for you."

"But I wasn't even there! I hadn't been there for days!"

"He didn't know you were staying with your Polack on the south side. You weren't home when he banged on your door, so he waited in his car. He wanted to talk to you. After a while, he left to have lunch with me."

"Poor Aaron. This is the second time he's been in the wrong place at the wrong time."

"Tell that to your detective. No, don't. He'll arrest me instead. Every time he looks at me, I feel like he's measuring me for handcuffs." Myer passed a shaking hand over his face and gingerly felt his jaw.

"He won't arrest you, Hank. Not after I tell him who killed Nanette."

"What?" Myer sat down on the bed and gripped her shoulders. "You know who killed her? Tell me, Max. She was my wife."

St. Clair hesitated. She wanted to make up for causing Hank so much pain by starting the whole investigation. She wanted to make up for making Hank find out from the police that his wife was poisoned. He deserved a kinder messenger—her. She wanted to tell Hank everything she knew. It didn't matter as far as the investigation anyway. As soon as Grabowski picked up his messages, he would call her. He would arrest the right person. It was practically over.

Hank smoothed the hair back from her forehead. The setting sun caught his dark hair, ringing it with a red glow.

"Who, Max?"

"I think she was killed by someone completely illogical. Nathan Schalz."

"Who?" Myer frowned. "I've never heard of him."

"Sure you have. The graduate student who shared my lab with me and Virginia."

"That hairy little creep? Are you crazy? Nanette treated him like a pet. At parties, she used to pat him on the head. Why would he kill her?"

"Why would anyone kill her? That's the question no one can answer. Nanette just wasn't that important for anyone to kill her. There's no motive for anyone. I'm only going on opportunity and means."

"Then it could be lots of people, including you. Why Nathan?"

"Nathan was the last person to see Nanette alive. He drove her back to her car on North Avenue after Aaron took her home. The prostitute who worked North Avenue with Nanette told me that she recognized Nathan in a photo I showed around the emergency room. Nathan had plenty of chances to steal the poison while we were using it in our research, and he had plenty of chances to give it to Nanette that night when he drove her back to her car."

Myer stood up and began to pace. "Did Virginia figure this out somehow and Nathan attacked her to keep her quiet?"

"Virginia is incredibly nosy. She probably saw Nathan and Nanette together in Nathan's lab one night. Nathan also knew Virginia was home this noon."

Myer clutched his hair. "That weird little freak killed my wife? I still can't believe it. Did you tell all this to your detective?"

St. Clair stared at the phone. "No, I can't reach Grabowski. I figured it all out while I was sitting here. I keep leaving messages for Grabowski, but until he calls me back, you and I are the only ones who know."

Myer grabbed his jacket. "I'm going to find out if this is true."

"Wait!" But the door had closed behind him. St. Clair flung herself against the pillows and pounded on the bed. What was Hank going to do if he found Nathan? Demand the truth? Then what? St. Clair wasn't even sure if she was right. She had no idea why Nathan would kill Nanette.

She thought about Nathan working in his lab, not knowing Hank was coming. She thought about Nathan stealing the tetrodotoxin and putting the chemical into a cola or a chocolate bar. She thought about Nathan sneaking into her own apartment to strangle her with a picture wire, Nathan hiding in Virginia's garage and hitting Virginia and her with a wrench. Did Nathan alter Virginia's test results to discredit her? Virginia had been blocking his Ph.D. for years. With Virginia dead or out of the way, Nathan could do his own research and move into Virginia's teaching position.

St. Clair watched the pigeons pecking on the window ledge. The facts fit, but the character didn't. Maxene had known Nathan for four years. They had shared a lab counter, shared equipment, lunch, confidences. She knew about his family, his hopes, what he ate, how he looked when he slept in his clothes. She knew his work habits and his approach to problems. She'd seen him at his lowest and his most jubilant, which for Nathan was one emotional degree apart.

Nathan was a patient, plodding researcher who never let one detail hang. Every drop of solvent was accounted for, every variation noted in every experiment. Where Virginia followed her flashes of intuition, Nathan followed his data. He was good, but not brilliant. He would never win the Nobel Prize because he lacked faith in his intuition. Nothing came to Nathan in a dream. If he dreamed, he discounted it, and followed a preset plan.

Was this the man who would steal a research chemical to murder a woman, then try to murder two others? Too much was left to chance.

Something was very wrong with her theory, including

the fact that she didn't know why Nathan would do any of this. Nanette was a collector of secrets; perhaps that was the answer. St. Clair thought through the people involved in Nanette's life on North Avenue: Hank, Aaron Simonson, Rolondo, Lavelle.

Lavelle. There was something about Lavelle that nagged at her. Something she had said or that St. Clair had noticed.

The phone number. St. Clair hadn't called the number the prostitute gave her the night before. She fumbled through her purse, spilling the contents out on the bed—her wallet, the photos she had been showing around the ER. She had scribbled the phone number on the back of one of the photos. She dialed the number. It was already evening; the woman might be out working the streets. The phone rang and rang. Then the woman answered.

"Hang on, honey," she said to St. Clair. "I'll find the number for you."

Pigeons were landing on the windowsill, crowding each other. St. Clair glanced at the photos spread over the bed. In her hand was the one with Nanette sitting on Aaron Simonson's lap, with Nathan and Virginia standing in the background. Was that the photo Lavelle was talking about?

"Here's the number, honey."

St. Clair scribbled it down. Then she stared at it, disbelieving. It was the phone number of Nathan's lab. The final piece of evidence pointing to him. But why did an inner-city prostitute have Nathan's number?

More pigeons landed, took off, landed, while St. Clair stared into space, waiting for the answer. The phone rang.

"Grabowski!" she shouted into the receiver.

"Kareena Singh," a quiet voice said.

Suddenly the answer was clear. St. Clair knew the connection, why Nanette was murdered, and how. One question to Kareena Singh verified it all.

"That's why I was calling," Kareena said in her soft voice. "I was wondering if you had noticed it, too?"

"I had," St. Clair said. "I just never put it together. I hope it isn't too late."

She put her finger on the receiver, then dialed Nathan's lab. The phone rang twenty times. No answer. She called police headquarters. Grabowski was still out. She climbed out of bed and pulled on her clothes.

A summer storm had come up, blackening the stars and moon from the sky. The air smelled of street dust and oil. Raindrops the size of quarters mixed with hail smacked into her windshield. The campus streetlights barely penetrated the storm.

In front of the lab, her headlights picked up a white Mercedes. It might be Hank's, but recognizing people's cars was a skill she had never mastered. Lots of doctors drove a white Mercedes.

The building lights were off, but flickers of lightning brightened the stairs. On the third floor, the smell of mice and guinea pigs brought an unaccountable lump to her throat. Sacrificing guinea pigs and white mice no longer seemed an acceptable way to find answers to human problems. It hadn't answered her digitalis hypothesis, and it hadn't answered Virginia's leprosy hypothesis.

Voices were coming from behind the closed door in Nathan's lab. She put an ear to the door. Then a voice spoke, so close to her she jumped and accidentally touched the door. It swung open slightly.

Hank Myer was standing a foot away, his back to the door. Over his shoulder, St. Clair could see Nathan and Virginia. Nathan's hairy face was drained of color and beads of sweat stood out on his mustache. His eyes were focused on whatever Hank held in his hand.

"I didn't kill your wife," Nathan said, his voice shaking. "The only time I ever went anywhere with her was the night she died. She called me here at the lab. She said her car had run out of gas and she needed a ride to the gas station. She wanted me to pick her up at your house."

"Why did she call you? You're a nothing!"

Nathan looked bewildered. "I don't know. She wanted to talk to Virginia, but I told her Virginia had gone home. She said she had already called there, and Virginia wasn't home.

It was about eleven at night. Then she asked if I would drive her to her car. What could I say?"

"So you picked her up at our house, and you killed her."

"No! I picked her up, yes, but we just took your gas can and poured some gas into her car. It was parked on Twenty-first and North Avenue. It never occurred to me until yesterday that that was the same night she died."

"You're lying, Schalz. You killed her because she found out something about you that you didn't want known. That was her specialty, finding out about people. Then she would hold it over the person until even a saint would want to strangle her. I don't really blame you, Schalz, but she was my wife, and I can't let a killer go free. With our legal system, you'll never see the inside of a jail."

He raised his hand. St. Clair could see he was holding a gun.

Nathan scuttled sideways toward Virginia. "Dr. Gaust, help me! He's going to shoot me!"

Virginia stepped away from his groping hands and smiled. "Don't come to me for help, Schalz. You've been a pain in the ass for too many years. I've kept you from getting a Ph.D. for as long as I could, but you kept hanging on here somehow, poking your nose into my research, trying to use my test results to get your grants and your Ph.D. It's all over for you, Schalz. He's going to shoot you."

St. Clair threw all her weight against the door. "No, he's not!" she yelled, slamming the door against Myer's back and following it with her body. Myer went down with a crash. His head hit the edge of the lab counter, and he slumped to the floor. The gun fell from his hand and slid across the floor.

Nathan reached for the gun, but Virginia was ahead of him. She jumped across the motionless body of Hank Myer and snatched the gun away from Nathan's fingers.

"Call the police," she said to St. Clair. She pointed the gun at Nathan.

"Good idea," St. Clair said, picking up the phone. "They'll

be very interested in reviewing a few of the papers you have hidden in your desk. They'll enjoy reading your reports on the thousands of dollars you spent on an invisible refrigeration unit and invisible mice."

Virginia shrugged. "The refrigerator is at my house."

"It isn't there any more than the mice are. I searched your house before your mysterious intruder beat me up with a wrench. I didn't find any mice, but I did find a few things the health department will find interesting. Syringes, test tubes with some interesting bacteria. Notebooks filled with lab data on human experiments with leprosy bacteria."

"You found no such thing."

"Let's call Detective Grabowski and have him look."

Virginia moved the gun to point at Maxene. "You killed her, Maxene. In the emergency room. That's what I told Hank, and that's what he believed until you handed him your little theory that Nathan killed her. But that's okay. I'll shoot you now, then when Hank wakes up, he can shoot Nathan. I'll say Nathan shot you, and I grabbed the gun away from him."

"Maxene," Nathan whispered. "Did you tell Dr. Myer that I killed his wife?"

"I made a mistake," St. Clair said, her eyes on the gun. "You didn't kill Nanette Myer. Virginia did. Nanette was a collector of secrets, and she stumbled upon the million-dollar secret that would ruin Virginia's career forever. It must have been a shock, Virginia, when Nanette walked into your little inner-city human laboratory disguised as a prostitute. Lavelle brought her, and Lavelle recognized you from a photo I showed her. I thought Lavelle saw Nathan in the photo, but she was talking about you."

"I haven't the faintest idea what you're talking about," Virginia said. Her eyes wavered at Nathan who was sidling toward the lab counter.

St. Clair moved an inch toward the wide open door. One big leap, and she would be out of range of Virginia's gun.

"What about those documented cases of leprosy that you treated with your experimental drug, Virginia?" St. Clair demanded. "I found the documentation in your house while you were hiding in the garage, waiting to turn on the engine to lure me in."

"You didn't go into my house. You came straight around the corner into the garage, where some intruder hit us both with a wrench."

Out of the corner of her eye, St. Clair could see Nathan reaching for a bottle on a shelf under the counter. She moved closer to the door, drawing Virginia's attention away from Nathan.

"It didn't happen that way, Virginia. When I called to say I was coming over, you thought I had figured out your whole ugly operation. As it happened, I hadn't. I only thought you were fictionalizing your lab data. But you went out to your car and turned it on to attract my attention. Then you tried to club me with a wrench. When you heard the police sirens, you gave yourself a little bang on the head and lay down behind the exhaust pipe. Good try, but you couldn't have been lying there all the time you claimed. There wasn't enough carbon monoxide in your blood. I saw the blood-chemistry report."

"You're not going to tell me I beat you up in your own flat."

"No, you hired that done. There are plenty of goons for hire in the inner city. But the ball machine—that was pure Virginia. I should have recognized your bizarre sense of humor." She moved closer to the door.

Virginia's attention wavered between St. Clair and Schalz. The gun moved from side to side. St. Clair felt the sweat break out on her forehead.

"Injecting humans with experimental live leprosy bacteria is a crime," St. Clair continued, "even if you're paying your laboratory humans well with your research funds. Prostitutes and drug addicts may be expendable to you, but they're still protected under the law. If anyone found out you were using people as white mice and giving them actual cases of leprosy, you'd be finished in the medical world. You'd also find yourself in prison."

"You sound like Nanette Myer," Virginia said. "Shooting off her mouth. Dropping by the lab and asking how the 'experiment' was going. Asking all about leprosy at doctor parties. Dropping comments at her pool party about a possible big breakthrough in my research. Calling me up to play tennis so she could pump me about my research. She was getting on my nerves."

"Lavelle brought her in to your North Avenue human laboratory one night, didn't she?" St. Clair asked. "That's how she found out what you were doing."

"Nanette walked in one night dressed up in that disgusting red wig and that tight skirt. I think she was as surprised to see me as I was to see her. I recognized her right away, but she pretended she didn't know me, so I played along."

"Did she know what you were doing?"

"Not the first time she came. I heard her asking the prostitutes she was with, but all they knew was that I paid them money to give them injections. What was one more needle mark to them?"

"How long did it take Nanette to figure out what you were doing?"

"About a week. She showed up in my lab at Marquette a week after I saw her on North Avenue, pretending she was between classes and wanted a cup of coffee. She hung around asking questions for a while. I spotted her a couple of times in the lab with Nathan, prying information out of him. Then, there she was again on Twenty-first and North, dressed up in that red wig and miniskirt, making sure she knew what was going on. In the meantime, she had to throw a party and make a lot of remarks about human experimentation."

St. Clair shifted her weight, getting herself closer to the door. She could see Nathan was holding a brown bottle. She forced herself to hold Virginia's gaze.

"So when Nanette came back to Twenty-first and North, you killed her," St. Clair said.

"I had the tetrodotoxin solution ready. I had always worried that Nathan would figure out who I was experimenting on, so I stole a few cc's of your solution, just in case I would have to use it on him. Nathan was always poking into my research, asking questions. I'm sure he searched my desk one night."

"So you handed Nanette a poisoned capsule, and she just ate it?"

"Of course. It looked like the one I gave to Lavelle. I paid the prostitutes to get the leprosy injection, and I paid them each time they took a capsule of my experimental drug. Nanette had come in with Lavelle enough times before that night so that she knew the routine. When she and Lavelle came in that night, I kept on pretending I didn't recognize her, and that I didn't know she had never received the initial dose of leprosy bacteria."

"But why would she take the pill? Why not refuse?"

"She was going along with playing the role, maybe. How should I know why she did what she did? She'd seen Lavelle take the pills before and never saw her have a bad reaction."

Nathan had taken the stopper off the brown bottle. St. Clair flexed her knees. She took a deep breath and jumped for the door.

The gun went off with an explosion. St. Clair screamed and collapsed on the floor of the hallway just outside the door. Out of the corner of her eye, she saw the brown bottle fly through the air and hit Virginia in the face. Virginia went over backward, out of St. Clair's line of vision.

Cautiously, St. Clair pulled herself to her knees. Nathan was sitting on Virginia, pouring liquid from the brown bottle onto her face, holding a handkerchief over her mouth. The room reeked of chloroform. St. Clair retched, sick with relief and nauseated by the chloroform. In a few seconds, Nathan was beside her, gasping.

"Call your detective," Nathan coughed. "Although there's no hurry. There's enough chloroform in that air to keep both those two under for hours."

CHAPTER

20

"POUR ME ANOTHER?" St. Clair asked. She held out her glass. "Full pitchers of beer spill when I pour with a bad arm."

Grabowski grinned. "Can you manage to drink it alone, or do you need help with that, too?" The amber liquid rose in her glass. A river of foam escaped down the side.

"I can get sloshed as easily drinking with the left hand as with the right." St. Clair toasted them.

Shirley and Kareena Singh returned the toast.

"I still don't understand how Dr. Gaust thought she could get away with it," Shirley said. "Injecting people with leprosy? What if someone actually got the disease?" She shuddered.

"They did," St. Clair said. "That was the whole idea. Virginia needed to treat actual leprosy cases to prove that her drug worked. Then she could take the drug and her fictitious mouse experiment data to the European drug company that was funding her, knowing she could safely take the drug to the test market. Europeans don't have the same restrictions on human experimentation as Americans, but all drug companies like to know they're working with a sure thing."

"But what if her drug hadn't worked? There would be leprosy cases all over the inner city!" Grabowski looked appalled.

Dr. Singh nodded. "There are, in fact. Virginia's victims had lots of bad habits, like exchanging needles, having sex indiscriminately, doing everything they could to pass on communicable diseases. I found a few more cases of leprosy on mothers who brought their babies to clinic. Dr. Gaust thought she was keeping track of all the people she had given injections to, but prostitutes tend to look the same, especially at night. Besides, the prostitutes themselves lied in order to get more money. They used each other's names to get repeated treatments before it was time. Others didn't get any treatment at all. None of them knew the risk they were taking since Virginia never actually told them which disease they were getting."

"Actually," St. Clair said, "the cases you picked up in clinic were people who never followed through with treatment. Virginia's drug actually does work. The drug company that funded her is going to make a fortune. But even if it hadn't worked, leprosy cases get treated quickly in this country. Public-health nurses are detectives, themselves, and people with unhealed sores get medical care eventually. I saw Lavelle's leprosy symptoms on her hands when she came into the ER. I didn't recognize it then, but I made the connection as soon as Kareena Singh told me on the phone that she was seeing more cases."

"That's why I called Max." Dr. Singh nodded. "Max takes care of the same inner-city population that I do. I wondered if she were seeing the same symptoms I was. I was fairly certain it was leprosy, since I'd seen it in India. It's not a sight a person forgets."

St. Clair nodded. "My great-aunt described it in her letters to me when I was a child, and after she retired she showed me pictures she took at the leper colony. I couldn't forget it either."

"Does this mean we're going to have an ER full of leprosy cases?" Shirley looked alarmed.

Dr. Singh shook her head. "We've put a special public-health team on this, and it won't take the public-health nurses long to find the cases and get treatment started. They track down VD and tuberculosis cases every day."

"What about Lavelle?" Shirley asked. "She left for Alabama with a case of leprosy."

"The Alabama state health department has been notified," Dr. Singh said.

Grabowski took St. Clair's hand. He sighed. "You figured this out because Lavelle told you to go to a certain place on Twenty-first and North Avenue, and you went there at night. The same night you went to Nathan's lab."

"It wasn't dangerous," St. Clair protested. "Two women walking down the street gave me a phone number to call, which turned out to be the number of Virginia's office. It's the same number for the lab, which really belonged to her since she was department head. Because of space limitations, the lab was also used by Nathan and me. The switchboard operator directed her calls either to her office or to the lab. It was risky for Virginia to give that number out, but she had to know if someone was having a bad reaction to her drug. She didn't want anyone going to an emergency room and spilling the whole story."

"Lucky thing you searched her house before you went into that garage," Shirley said.

St. Clair smiled. "Breaking and entering is a crime. I guessed the lab data and supplies were in there, but I never saw them."

"Speaking of research," Kareena Singh said, "have you decided whether you're going back into research or sticking with the real world?"

"I spoke to the dean this morning," St. Clair said. "He's finding a replacement for me for another year. He agrees that one year isn't long enough for a woman to decide what to do with her life, so he approved another year's leave of absence."

The bartender's bellow broke through the cheers that met St. Clair's announcement. "Grabowski! Order of fish fries!" Shirley pounded Maxene on the back, then put a heavy hand on Grabowski's shoulder and heaved herself to her feet.

"I'll get the fish, honey," Shirley said. "I'm trying to get something going with that bartender. Don't expect your food real soon."

"In that case, I'm going for a rest stop," Kareena said, gracefully disentangling her sari from the table legs.

Grabowski moved his chair closer to St. Clair and took her hand. He leaned his elbows on the table and held her fingers to his lips. His mustache brushed her hand softly while he spoke.

"When are you coming back to live with me again?" he murmured. "I've hired a cleaning lady, and the painters are coming next week. I'm even getting the porch repaired."

St. Clair smiled. "You're so romantic, Grabowski. Some days I actually miss that bare light bulb in the kitchen and the sandy linoleum."

"The cleaning lady hung a Japanese lantern on the bulb."

St. Clair rubbed her face against his shoulder. The soft cotton shirt smelled like a Milwaukee summer—fish fries and sweat, with a brandy chaser. "You're talking about change. I don't want you to change. I'm not sure I can handle your domestic habits at continuous close quarters, but I'm fond of them. I wouldn't like you if you changed."

"Then I'll buy a bigger place and each of us can live in half. We'll meet in the bedroom."

She smiled. "Now you're tempting me. Keep it up and one of these days I'll say yes."

Four baskets of fish fries plunked down on the table. Shirley dragged up her chair.

"I've got me a live one," she announced, jerking her head at the grinning bartender. "He's going back to law school. Can you beat that? Man of his age? And he's looking for an educated woman to team up with, he says. He probably means he wants a meal ticket. What do you think? Should a grown man go back to school?"

"What do you think, Grabowski?" St. Clair smiled. "Should a forty-year-old, good-looking, smart man with a job that he's good at give it all up and go to law school?"

"As it happens," Grabowski began, "I've been giving that a lot of thought. I've decided that there are already plenty of lawyers. Next year would be just as good as this one for making a big decision like that."

About the Author

Janet McGiffin lives in Olympia, Washington, and Tel Aviv, Israel. *Emergency Murder* is her first mystery.